Samuel French Acting Edition

I0591869

Jack of Diamonds

by Marcia Kash &
Douglas E. Hughes

SAMUELFRENCH.COM   SAMUELFRENCH.CO.UK

FOR PRODUCTION ENQUIRIES

UNITED STATES AND CANADA
Info@SamuelFrench.com
1-866-598-8449

UNITED KINGDOM AND EUROPE
Plays@SamuelFrench.co.uk
020-7255-4302

Each title is subject to availability from Samuel French, depending upon country of performance. Please be aware that *JACK OF DIAMONDS* may not be licensed by Samuel French in your territory. Professional and amateur producers should contact the nearest Samuel French office or licensing partner to verify availability.

MUSIC USE NOTE

Licensees are solely responsible for obtaining formal written permission from copyright owners to use copyrighted music in the performance of this play and are strongly cautioned to do so. If no such permission is obtained by the licensee, then the licensee must use only original music that the licensee owns and controls. Licensees are solely responsible and liable for all music clearances and shall indemnify the copyright owners of the play(s) and their licensing agent, Samuel French, against any costs, expenses, losses and liabilities arising from the use of music by licensees. Please contact the appropriate music licensing authority in your territory for the rights to any incidental music.

IMPORTANT BILLING AND CREDIT REQUIREMENTS

If you have obtained performance rights to this title, please refer to your licensing agreement for important billing and credit requirements.

JACK OF DIAMONDS was first produced at Theatre Aquarius in Hamilton, Ontario, Canada. It opened on October 30, 2015. The production was directed by Ron Ulrich, with set and costume design by Ivan Brozic, lighting design by Louise Guinand, and sound design by Anna-Maria Steger. The stage manager was Josephine Ho and the assistant stage manager was Kimberly Brown. The cast was as follows:

JACK NEWMAN	Ian D. Clark
ROSE	Wendy Thatcher
WILF/MORTIMER/POLICEMAN	Neil Foster
BLANCHE	Mary Long
FLORA	Valerie Boyle
NURSE HARPER	Catherine Fitch
BARNEY EFFWARD	Derek McGrath

CHARACTERS

JACK NEWMAN – Late sixties to seventies. A successful businessman, former jeweller and late-night TV pitchman, physically spry, still very much engaged in life.

ROSE – Late sixties to seventies. An independent, feisty old bird, a real technophile.

BLANCHE – Late sixties. A fading beauty, suffers from narcolepsy.

FLORA – Late sixties to early seventies. Grandmotherly type, always cheerful, very talented at making jewelry, has memory issues.

NURSE HARPER – Forty to fifty-five. Career nurse, lonely, unappreciated, bored, and frustrated.

BARNEY EFFWARD – Forty-five to sixty. Charming con man. A Bernie Madoff type.

MORTIMER – Mid-forties. Uptight, hypochondriac lawyer.

WILF GUNNARSON – Eighty-nine years old. Almost completely deaf but totally with it.

POLICEMAN – Forties, straight-laced, humorless. A real by-the-book type.

*Please note: Wilf, Mortimer, and Policeman may be played by the same actor.

SETTING

Transitions Retirement Home, a comfortable and expensive home for seniors.

TIME

The present.

ACKNOWLEDGEMENTS

The authors would like to thank Ron Ulrich and Theatre Aquarius for the support and development of this piece.

In addition, they would like to extend special thanks to their friend and colleague Jamie Farr for his invaluable contribution, support, and enthusiasm in bringing *Jack of Diamonds* to fruition.

ACT I

Scene I

*(**SETTING:** The common room of Transitions Retirement Villa, an old folks' home in an urban center. In the upstage right corner is an archway leading to the main entrance. On the opposite corner upstage left there is an archway leading to the dining room, kitchen, and other common areas. On the wall upstage center are three doors leading to bedrooms. On the stage left wall is a door leading to a closet. Below this, also on the stage left wall, is a door leading to a bathroom. On the stage right wall is a window with a window seat. Next to this is a bookshelf containing books, games, DVD's, etc. Downstage center is a sofa. Downstage right is an armchair with a side table next to it. The remains of a cake sit on the table. Downstage is a table and four chairs. Unseen, on the fourth wall downstage center, is a large flat-screen television. At rise, four of the residents – **JACK, FLORA, ROSE,** and **WILF** – are seated at the table downstage left playing euchre. **JACK** is a feisty, retired jeweller and TV pitchman in his sixties. **FLORA** is a pleasant, grandmotherly type. **ROSE** has a cane parked next to her. She wears a pair of very thick-rimmed glasses which are currently on the top of her head, and she pays less attention to the game than to the iPad in her lap. **WILF** sports a pair of hearing aids. Across the upstage wall hangs a banner that reads, "Farewell Wilf!")*

JACK. Hey Rose, we're trying to play cards here. Enough with the twitting.

ROSE. Tweeting.

JACK. It's annoying, whatever you call it. Play a card already.

ROSE. *(Typing furiously.)* Just give me a minute.

JACK. *(Indicating WILF.)* Wilf's eighty-nine years old. He doesn't *have* a minute!

WILF. Eh?

JACK. Just play something. Anything.

> *(ROSE puts a card on the table.)*

ROSE. There.

JACK. That's a spade, Rose. Clubs are led.

ROSE. Really?

> *(She picks the card up and inspects it, then remembers she's not wearing her glasses. She puts them on and inspects the card very closely.)*

Oh, so they are. My mistake. Well, I don't have any of those, so I'll just play this.

> *(She puts another card down.)*

There.

JACK. Aw, Rose, you trumped my damn ace!

ROSE. I did? I'm so sorry.

> *(BLANCHE enters from her room upstage left. She's an attractive, stylishly dressed woman, appearing to be a bit on the young side for a retirement home. There's an air of the fading beauty about her.)*

BLANCHE. Good evening, all!

JACK. *(Brightening as he sees her.)* There you are!

ROSE. *(Overlapping.)* Good evening, Blanche.

FLORA. Hello, Blanche.

BLANCHE. Sorry I'm late. I must have nodded off. Did I miss your party, Wilf?

> *(She bends down and gives WILF a kiss on the cheek.)*

Things just won't be the same around here without you.

WILF. Eh?

BLANCHE. Any cake left?

JACK. On the table over there. Let me get you a slice.

> *(He starts to get up, and* **BLANCHE** *puts a hand on his shoulder.)*

BLANCHE. Don't fuss, I can manage.

> *(She gives him a kiss on the lips. He pulls her onto his lap.)*

ROSE. Aw, look at that. Aren't they sweet?

WILF. I guess you're never too old to get one of Cupid's arrows in your ass. Why don't you two get a room?

JACK. *(Loudly.)* We tried that. But they won't give us one unless we're married.

BLANCHE. And neither of us wants to go *that* route again.

> *(She helps herself to some cake.)*

> *(Indicating the card game.)* So, who's winning?

JACK. Not us.

> *(***BLANCHE*** sits down on the sofa and eats her cake.* ***ROSE****'s iPad beeps. She takes off her glasses and examines the screen. She's aghast at what she reads.)*

ROSE. Oh, you little poop! I'll show you...

> *(She begins typing furiously.)*

JACK. Oh for cryin' out loud, Rose! Are you playing the game or aren't you?

ROSE. I'm sorry Jack, but I can't let some pipsqueak from Nebraska try to tell me he's getting 11.5 megabytes per second with a cable internet connection!

WILF. Eh?

> *(She goes back to her typing.)*

JACK. Could I have that in English, please?

ROSE. Just a second – W, T, F, question mark, question mark, question mark, exclamation point!

JACK. Just play a card, Rose!

ROSE. Sorry. Now where did I put my glasses?

JACK. They're on your damn head.

ROSE. *(Putting them on.)* Oh, for heaven's sake.

FLORA. Rose dear, I don't understand why you keep taking your glasses off to look at your whatchamacallit – your maxi pad.

ROSE. iPad, Flora.

FLORA. How can you make anything out on that little screen?

ROSE. I have a new app.

BLANCHE. Eh?

FLORA. Eh?

WILF. Eh?

ROSE. An app. It's called "iZBad."

> *(Pronounced "eyes bad.")*

It's for people with poor eyesight, like me. You just enter your prescription, and it adjusts the screen so you can read it without your glasses.

BLANCHE. My goodness, how –

> *(She falls asleep, her head dropping to her chest.)*

JACK. How – useful?

FLORA. Handy?

ROSE. Clever?

BLANCHE. *(Waking up and continuing, unaware she was asleep.)* Clever.

ROSE. Bingo! I win again!

> *(She holds out her hand and* **FLORA** *and* **JACK** *each give her a dollar.)*

Wow! That's five bucks since breakfast.

JACK. I don't have any time for all these new contraptions. People are so busy texting and twitting they're completely unaware of what's going on in the world around them.

(Pointedly.)

Like this card game.

(He taps the table.)

ROSE. Oh, is it still me? Sorry.

(As she plays a card.)

There you go.

*(The others follow suit. **WILF** is last.)*

WILF. Euchre!

JACK. Aaaghh!

(He throws down his cards in disgust.)

FLORA. That's ten points for us. One more game for the good guys!

(Gathering the cards.)

Shall we play another?

JACK. *(Getting up from the table.)* No, I'm done. You want to take over for me, Blanche?

(He looks over and sees that she's asleep.)

Oops, she's gone again.

ROSE. That's one weird affliction.

FLORA. What is?

ROSE. Narcolepsy.

FLORA. Who's got narcolepsy?

JACK. *(With a sigh.)* Flora.

FLORA. I've got narcolepsy?

ROSE. No, Flora, not you – *Blanche!*

*(Noticing the bracelet on **FLORA**'s wrist.)*

Oh, that's a nice piece, when did you make that?

FLORA. *(Showing it off.)* Thanks, I just finished it last night.

WILF. Those stones are pretty. They must have set you back a few bucks.

FLORA. Not really. I get them for cheap at Walmart.

JACK. *(Taking her wrist and inspecting the bracelet.)* That's really nice work, Flora. You know, in my day, I could have sold this for five hundred bucks, easy.

FLORA. Five hundred dollars? For this?

JACK. Sure.

FLORA. *(Confidentially.)* They're not real diamonds, you know.

JACK. Of course not. If these were real, you'd be looking at five figures at least.

FLORA. My goodness!

ROSE. You've got a serious talent there, Flora. I keep telling you, you could turn this into a business.

FLORA. Oh, I wouldn't know where to begin. Besides, you can't exactly open a jewelry store in this place, can you?

ROSE. Of course you can. Just do it online.

FLORA. Oh, I really wouldn't know how to do that!

ROSE. You wouldn't have to. I could do it for you. You'd need your own website, of course, but that's a snap. We could upload pictures of your stuff, then it's just a matter of setting up an account with PayPal, making arrangements with the major credit cards, and hooking up with UPS or somebody like that for the shipping –

FLORA. Oh heavens. It all sounds much too complicated. I could never keep track. Besides, it would take all the fun out of it if I made it a full-time job. And it's not like I need the money.

ROSE. No indeed. We're all set for life, thanks to Barney.

FLORA. Who?

ROSE. You know, dear – Barney, Barney Effward. That nice man Jack introduced us to. The one who's handling our investments now.

FLORA. Oh, yes. *That* Barney.

JACK. *(Teasing.)* Yeah, your boyfriend.

FLORA. Oh, you.

ROSE. You're blushing, Flora.

FLORA. I am not. You know, he told me I looked just like Elizabeth Taylor.

WILF. Who?

ROSE. *(Loudly.)* Elizabeth Taylor, dear.

JACK. He said *Flora* looks like Elizabeth Taylor?

WILF. *(To JACK.)* He musta been wearing Rose's glasses.

       (**JACK** *chuckles.*)

FLORA. I wonder when he'll be coming to see us again. I want to give him that tie clip I made for him.

WILF. Eh?

ROSE. *(Loudly.)* A tie clip, dear.

JACK. See? Told you she had the hots for him.

      (**WILF** *chuckles.*)

FLORA. *(Smiling.)* Oh, stop. I just wanted to thank him for everything he's done for us.

ROSE. Yes, he's been a godsend, hasn't he?

WILF. Too bad Barney didn't show up when I still had something in the bank. If I'd known I was going to live this long, I would have been more careful with my money.

JACK. *(Patting* **WILF** *on the shoulder.)* I'm sure going to miss you.

WILF. No you're not. You're going to love it. Now that I'm leaving you won't have any competition. You're going to have these ladies beating a path to your bedroom door.

ROSE. Oh, Wilf, you're such a dirty old man.

WILF. You're just figuring that out now? I've been a dirty old man since I was twelve.

      (**NURSE HARPER,** *a severe-looking woman in her forties, enters from upstage right.)*

HARPER. Still here, are we boys and girls? It's well past nine o'clock.

JACK. So, what, we've got a bedtime now?

HARPER. Now Mr. Newman, you know very well that this room was only reserved for Mr. Gunnarson's party until nine o'clock.

> *(As she crosses to the banner upstage center and begins to take it down.)*

We have to consider the needs of the other residents.

JACK. At this time of night, their only needs are a glass for their teeth and a night light.

HARPER. *(Ignoring him and crossing to the cake.)* I take it we're all done with this?

> *(As she goes to pick up the cake, she notices that the sleeping* BLANCHE *has dropped her empty plate on the couch. She crosses to pick it up and starts brushing the crumbs off the couch.)*

Tch, tch, tch. Now, this is why we like to have all our meals in the dining room. Then we don't have to worry about little messes everywhere.

JACK. *(Sotto voce.)* Oh, for God's sake.

> *(*HARPER *finds an empty liquor bottle down the side of the couch.)*

HARPER. *(Holding up the bottle.)* Who is responsible for this?

> *(Silence.)*

You know the rules, boys and girls. No liquor on the premises. Now to whom does this belong?

> *(Another silence.)*

I see. In that case I am going to have to report this to Dr. Anderson.

JACK. What's he going to do, ground us?

HARPER. *(Pointedly.)* Very possibly. He may just decide to cancel next week's trip to the Play With Your Food Dinner Theatre.

JACK. What? Miss out on a second-rate buffet while watching some third-rate comedy starring some fourth-rate has-been?

HARPER. Well it might not be much of a loss to you, Mr. Newman, but there are others here who look forward to these outings. The fact is, the rules are here for a reason and when you break them, there are consequences.

(She turns to leave.)

JACK. Ja, ja, mein Herr.

(JACK puts one finger under his nose like a mustache and performs a Nazi salute with his other arm.)

HARPER. It's like dealing with four-year-olds.

(Muttering under her breath as she exits.)

How did I end up in this godforsaken place anyway? I'm *so* overqualified for this job…

(ROSE and FLORA giggle as HARPER exits upstage left.)

JACK. Poor Nurse Harper. She needs to find a job where she can put her people skills to better use; like in a morgue.

WILF. What did she have to say?

JACK. *(Loudly.)* She wanted to make sure we give you a good send off. Here.

(JACK opens the window seat and pulls out a full bottle of single malt.)

Let's have a toast to Wilf, shall we?

FLORA. Hear hear. I'll get the cups.

(She exits into the bathroom and returns with a bunch of Dixie cups. Under the following JACK pours each of them a snort and passes out the cups.)

BLANCHE. *(Waking up.)* I must have dozed off.

(Looks at her watch.)

Oh, it's almost time for the news.

(She picks up the remote and turns on the TV. A loud commercial blares out. She struggles to try and turn on the mute.)

BLANCHE. *(Cont.)* Oh where is that silly mute button, I can never find it.

(She finds it and turns off the sound.)

There. Now, what did I miss?

JACK. Just a visit from the SS.

(Adopting a silly German accent.)

You will obey zee rules, or zere will be NO CRAPPY DINNER THEATRE for YOU!

ROSE. Your timing's perfect, Blanche. Here.

(She hands BLANCHE a cup.)

JACK. *(Holding up his Dixie cup, loudly.)* Here's to you Wilf, and to your new life at Departure Point. May you give them so much grief that they have no choice but to send you back!

WILF. Thanks, Jack.

(They down their drinks.)

Mmmm. You always get the good stuff.

JACK. *(Giving him the bottle.)* Here. Take it with you. You won't be seeing any of this where you're going.

(WILF lets out a big sigh. There is a beat.)

WILF. Well, I better go finish my packing. See you in the morning.

(They all ad-lib their various good nights. WILF exits.)

BLANCHE. It's so sad, his having to leave like this.

FLORA. I wish there was something we could do.

ROSE. Maybe there is.

FLORA. What do you mean?

ROSE. Well, we're all in pretty good shape –

(Looking around at them all.)

– financially speaking, that is. We could pool our resources and let Wilf live out the rest of his days here at Transitions with us.

BLANCHE. That's a lovely idea.

JACK. *(Appalled.)* Now just a minute. We're going to use *our* money to keep Wilf here? We can't do that. That's... that's socialism!

ROSE. No, that's helping out a friend. Socialism is sending him to a government facility.

FLORA. Exactly. Poor Wilf. That Departure Point is vile.

ROSE. All those government places are. The walls are always painted that sickly color of green and everything smells of pee.

JACK. Look, the whole reason Wilf's getting the boot is that he's outlived his savings. If we all start pitching in to rescue him we could end up in the same predicament.

BLANCHE. We could easily afford it between the four of us.

ROSE. Since we started with Barney, we've been getting a thirty percent return on our investment.

JACK. You can't count on things staying that way. The market is volatile as hell right now. If I had my druthers I'd be putting everything I have in precious stones.

ROSE. You sound like one of your commercials. Always trying to buy people's jewelry. What was the line, Jack? Come on, say it for us.

JACK. No.

ROSE. Come on, say it for us. Just once.

JACK. No.

BLANCHE. I can do it for you.

> *(Picking up a handful of cards from the table, and waving them in* **FLORA**'s *face.)*

"Have I got a DEAL for YOU!!"

> (**JACK** *snorts in disgust.*)

FLORA. *(Delighted.)* Oh yes, I remember those commercials.

> *(Beat.)*

FLORA. *(Cont.)* They were terrible.

> (**JACK** *rolls his eyes.*)

ROSE. Yes they were, but they made Jack a rich man.

JACK. Not that rich.

ROSE. Come on Jack, you'll never be in danger of going broke.

JACK. I will if my kids have their way. They don't want to wait for their inheritance, the greedy little buggers. They want my money now.

FLORA. Your own children?

BLANCHE. It's true.

FLORA. It's so…mercenary.

JACK. They can't help it. It's hereditary – they get it from their mother. Anyway, if they're not careful I might just give it all to charity.

BLANCHE. That's exactly what we're suggesting, Jack. Except in this case the charity is Wilf.

ROSE. Yes, wouldn't you rather spend your money on him than leave it to your greedy kids to fight over?

JACK. I don't want to spend it, period.

BLANCHE. I think it's a brilliant idea. I'm in.

FLORA. Me too. I have no children to provide for. I'd be happy to pitch in.

ROSE. Me three. So what do you say, Jack?

JACK. I dunno. It's still a bit commie pinko for my taste.

BLANCHE. Don't worry ladies, I know how to talk him into it.

ROSE. How?

BLANCHE. That's my secret.

JACK. *(Eyes lighting up.)* Secret? You mean…Victoria's Secret?

BLANCHE. *(Toying suggestively with her blouse.)* I might.

JACK. OK, I'm in.

BLANCHE. *(To* **ROSE** *and* **FLORA.***)* Works every time!

FLORA. Ooh, I can't wait to give Wilf the good news!

BLANCHE. Speaking of news, I just want to catch the headlines before we call it a night.

> (**BLANCHE** *aims the remote at the TV and turns up the sound.*)

NEWSCASTER. *(Voice-over.)* …and in our lead story, North American stock markets tumbled sharply this afternoon on the news that investment guru Barney Effward has been arrested for running a Ponzi scheme.

BLANCHE. Barney Effward?

ROSE. That's our Barney!

FLORA. *(Stricken.)* What's he doing in handcuffs?

NEWSCASTER. *(Voice-over.)* Effward, seen as something of a wunderkind in financial circles, was arrested today on hundreds of counts of fraud for allegedly bilking his clients – many of them senior citizens – out of millions of dollars.

JACK. Sonofabitch…

NEWSCASTER. *(Voice-over.)* In a dramatic turn of events, Effward collapsed in court this afternoon while being arraigned. He was immediately rushed to hospital. There is no word yet on his condition. In other news –

> (**BLANCHE** *turns off the TV. They all sit, stunned.*)

FLORA. What does this mean?

JACK. Well, for one thing, it means Wilf's moving out after all.

ROSE. Yes, and it looks like we'll be right behind him.

BLANCHE. You mean we're all going to have to move out?

JACK. We won't have any choice, sweetheart. As of right now, we're all flat broke.

> (*The lights fade to black.*)

Scene II

*(The next morning. **ROSE** sits at the table following
the story on her iPad. **JACK** is pacing, watching
the 24-hour news channel on the TV. The sound is
low. **FLORA** also sits at the table, working on one
of her jewelry pieces. **BLANCHE** sits on the window
seat, talking on the phone.)*

BLANCHE. No honey, I've already talked to both your
brothers. They say they just can't help... I know you
can't afford this place, darling, but you and Jeffrey do
have that spare room, at least until the baby comes...
Oh, I see... It's just that I'm only paid up until the end
of the month and I have nowhere else to go...

JACK. *(Who overhears some of this, disgustedly.)* Kids.

BLANCHE. No, no, it's alright, I understand. I'll be fine... I
love you too. Goodbye.

*(She hangs up and begins to cry. **JACK** crosses to
comfort her.)*

I'm going to end up at Departure Point!

JACK. Aw, don't cry, sweetheart.

BLANCHE. *(In tears.)* I don't want to live in a place that
smells like pee!

JACK. Don't worry. We'll find a way out of this.

FLORA. *(Decisively.)* I'm not going to one of those
government places. I'm staying right here.

JACK. And how are you going to manage that? You're flat
broke.

FLORA. Not for long.

(Holding up the piece of jewelry.)

You said I could sell one of these for – how much did
he say, Rose?

ROSE. Five hundred bucks. We've got it all worked out,
Jack. Once the website's finished, all we have to do is

sell five of these a week, and the two of us can make enough to stay here.

JACK. Five a week, eh? How long does it take you to make one of those, Flora?

FLORA. *(Pleasantly.)* A few days. If my arthritis isn't acting up.

JACK. Well that's not going to work, is it?

(**FLORA** *looks at* **ROSE**, *confused.*)

ROSE. *(Defensively.)* It's a start. At least we're doing something constructive.

(Typing on her iPad.)

There. I've secured our domain name – geriatricjewelry dot com. If all goes well, we should have the website up and running in a few days.

FLORA. Then I'd better get cracking.

ROSE. Anyway, this Barney business isn't over yet. Let's just wait and see what's left of his assets. We might get something back.

(**JACK** *snorts.*)

You know what these crooks are like. They've always got private jets and yachts and such things. Once it's been liquidated that stuff will be worth millions.

JACK. And once all the lawyers get paid, how much of it do you think we're going to see?

ROSE. There will be loot stuffed away somewhere.

(The iPad beeps. **ROSE** *takes her glasses off to read.)*

Oh no!

JACK. What is it?

ROSE. It's all over Twitter. They've had a look at Barney's books, and he sold off everything he owned months ago. They've checked his bank accounts too.

JACK. Don't tell me. Empty.

FLORA. What a snake!

ROSE. That's an insult to snakes.

JACK. This is all my fault. I'm the one who introduced him to you.

ROSE. Now, now, Jack. Don't go blaming yourself. I mean, he talked a great game. We were all duped. And it wasn't just us, remember. He managed to swindle major charities, brokerage firms, high-end investors. We're in very good company.

JACK. Doesn't make us any the less broke. The bottom line is, because of *me* none of us can afford to stay here any more.

> (*A beat as they ponder their collective fate.* ROSE *points at the TV screen.*)

ROSE. Looks like there's something happening.

> (JACK *grabs the remote and turns up the volume. From the TV, we hear the sounds of sirens and much crowd noise.*)

REPORTER. (*Voice-over.*) The scene outside St. Genesius Hospital is one of pandemonium. Some time overnight, word leaked out on social media that Barney Effward was being treated here, and a large crowd of angry investors quickly gathered and stormed the hospital, threatening to kill him.

ROSE. Good for them! String him up by the short and curlies!

FLORA. Yes, string him up!

> (*Beat.*)

Who are we talking about again?

REPORTER. (*Voice-over.*) A police spokesperson announced a few moments ago that Effward had been removed from the hospital for his own safety. The question now is where is Barney Effward and will he survive until his next court appearance? This is Chuck Williams for Eyewitness News.

> (JACK *turns down the volume on the TV.*)

ROSE. *(Reading from her iPad.)* It says here that there were over a hundred people at the hospital. Some of them had weapons!

JACK. More power to them, I say.

FLORA. Wish I'd known, I'd have been at the head of the line with my Glock!

ROSE. Oh Flora, you don't have a Glock.

JACK. Where did they take him? Does it say?

ROSE. No...all it says is "an undisclosed location."

JACK. Well they better keep it undisclosed, or Barney's a dead man.

> *(NURSE HARPER enters from upstage right, pushing a man in a wheelchair. The man sports a watch cap and sunglasses. A scarf is around his neck.)*

HARPER. Excuse me, everyone. May I have your attention, please?

> *(BLANCHE wakes up.)*

JACK. *(Snapping to attention.)* Achtung!

HARPER. *(With a look to JACK.)* I'd like to introduce you to our new guest. Mister...Smith will only be staying with us temporarily.

JACK. Join the club.

ROSE. What's wrong with him? He looks like he's in a coma or something.

HARPER. He's not in a coma, he's just non-responsive.

FLORA. Non-responsive?

JACK. Sounds like my ex-wife.

> *(We hear the sound of a bell, followed by a tinny VOICE on an intercom.)*

VOICE. *(Offstage.)* Lunch is now being served in the dining room. Today's menu is tomato rice soup, corned beef and cabbage followed by butterscotch pudding!

> *(There is a collective groan from the residents.)*

VOICE. *(Cont.)* Bone appeteet.

> *(There is a clunk as the intercom is turned off. The residents begin to make their way to the dining room.)*

BLANCHE. I don't think I could eat a thing.

JACK. Come on now, Blanche, you gotta get something down you.

> *(The women exit upstage left.* **JACK** *begins to usher* **BLANCHE** *out.)*

HARPER. Er, Mr. Newman. Could I have a word with you, please?

JACK. *(To* **BLANCHE.***)* Save me a seat, honey. I'll be right there.

> *(***JACK** *turns back to* **HARPER.***)*

What can I do for you?

HARPER. It's about the sleeping arrangements for Mr. Smith. As we have no available beds at the moment, he will be bunking in with you.

JACK. What? You can't just stick him in with me without my permission!

HARPER. I think if you examine your contract more closely, you'll discover that we can. Besides, there's nowhere else to put him.

JACK. Why don't you give him Wilf's room?

HARPER. Mr. Gunnarson's room has already been taken.

JACK. Well there's gotta be somewhere else he can go!

HARPER. I can't put him in with one of the women, Mr. Newman. And now that Mr. Gunnarson has left us, you are the only male resident here.

JACK. Why don't you stick him in with Mrs. Draper? She's almost a man.

HARPER. Mr. Newman, please!

JACK. And just how long am I supposed to put up with this?

HARPER. It's only for a few days. And what's more, you're going to keep quiet about it too.

JACK. Keep quiet about what?

HARPER. There's something I need to show you.

> (**HARPER** *removes the hat and sunglasses from the man in the wheelchair to reveal a catatonic man in middle age.*)

JACK. Holy crap, it's Barney Effward!

HARPER. Ssh!!

> (*Quietly.*)

That's *Mr. Smith* to you.

JACK. What the hell is that bastard doing here?

HARPER. They needed to put him in a safe place where his victims wouldn't think to look for him.

JACK. So they brought him *here?*

HARPER. Look, I'm no happier about this than you are; but orders are orders. I've been given the job of taking care of him, and unfortunately for both of us, I can't do that without your help.

JACK. Well I don't care what you say. He's not sharing a room with me.

HARPER. Oh yes he is – and what's more, you're going to keep his identity to yourself.

JACK. Why would I want to do that? What's to stop me from picking up the phone and telling the world where he is?

HARPER. This!

> (*She pulls out a piece of official-looking paper from her pocket.*)

JACK. What's that?

HARPER. A subpoena. Your children's lawyer has ordered me to appear at your competency hearing.

JACK. Competency hearing? What are you talking about?

HARPER. Didn't your lawyer notify you? Your children have applied to have you declared legally incompetent.

JACK. What??

HARPER. They say you're a danger to yourself and others and they want power of attorney over you.

JACK. Look, that was all a misunderstanding! I just got my prescriptions mixed up. It only happened the once.

HARPER. They're very concerned for your safety.

JACK. What a bunch of crap! They couldn't care less about my safety. They're just trying to get their hands on my money.

HARPER. Power of attorney doesn't just give them control over your money, Mr. Newman. It gives them control over every aspect of your life.

JACK. Meaning?

HARPER. Meaning, for example, they may decide that this isn't the safest place for you. They may want you transferred to a more secure facility.

JACK. What are you saying? They'd stick me in some padded cell somewhere?

HARPER. Exactly. With a big lock – on the outside.

JACK. They can't do that!

HARPER. Oh yes they can. And whether or not they do will depend to a large degree on what I have to say to the judge.

(*Indicating* **BARNEY**.)

Now, I've been instructed to keep this man comfortable for a few days and to keep him incognito. If you choose to assist me I can help make this little problem –

(*Holding up the subpoena.*)

– go away. If not –

(*Mimes turning a deadbolt, along with the appropriate sound effect.*)

So. Do we understand one another?

(**JACK**, *seething, says nothing.*)

I'll take that as a yes.

(*The intercom clicks on.*)

VOICE. *(Offstage.)* Nurse Harper to reception. Nurse Harper to reception.

HARPER. I'll be right back. And remember, your future is in my hands.

*(She hands him **BARNEY**'s hat, scarf, and glasses and exits upstage right.)*

JACK. *(Throwing the stuff on the floor.)* Competency hearing? If anybody needs a competency hearing it's YOU, you conniving little…keep him incognito? After what he's done? He'll be lucky if I keep him alive!

*(He glares at **BARNEY**, who stares into space.)*

What are you looking at?

(No response.)

You can quit the Madame Tussauds act now. It's just you and me, buddy.

(No reaction.)

Come on F-word, cut the crap. Collapsing in the middle of your arraignment? You may have fooled the judge with that stunt but you're not fooling me.

(No reaction.)

Tch. Some financial wizard you turned out to be! I can't believe I fell for that sales pitch of yours. What have you got to say for yourself, you sonofa…

(No reaction.)

(With mounting frustration.) Come on, speak!! You heard what the Commandant said. I've got to keep your dirty little secret, so you might as well talk. Go ahead – say something!

*(**JACK** gives him a shove. **BARNEY** wobbles a little but says nothing.)*

Hmm.

*(**JACK** shoves him again. **BARNEY** wobbles again but still no reaction.)*

JACK. *(Cont.)* Nah, this can't be for real.

> *(He lifts BARNEY's arm and lets go. It flops down.)*

Okay, maybe this will wake you up!

> *(He suddenly picks up a glass of water and throws its contents in BARNEY's face. No reaction.)*

What did they do at that hospital, shoot you full of Thorazine?

> *(A beat as he looks closely at BARNEY.)*

Hmm. Maybe a physical examination is in order.

> *(He tickles BARNEY's ribs.)*

Tickle, tickle, tickle.

> *(No reaction.)*

Alright. Let's try your other funny bone. So, a guy goes to the doctor, doctor says, "You've got six months to live." The guy says, "I can't pay my bill." So the doc says, "Okay, you've got another six months."

> *(No response.)*

Didn't like that one, eh? How about this? Doctor says to me, "You'll live to be seventy!" I tell him "I AM SEVENTY!" Doc says, "See, what did I tell you?"

> *(No response.)*

Hmm. Tough room. Okay, here's my favorite: guy goes to the doctor with a duck growing out of the top of his head. Doctor says, "How on earth did that happen?" The duck says, "Would you believe it started as a pimple on my ass?"

> *(He cracks himself up, throwing his arms in the air as FLORA, ROSE, and BLANCHE enter from upstage left and stop short at what they are seeing.)*

BLANCHE. Jack!

> *(JACK freezes in some awkward pose.)*

JACK. Agh!

BLANCHE. What are you doing?

(**JACK** *steps in front of* **BARNEY** *in an attempt to hide him and does his best Bruce Lee imitation.*)

JACK. Hi-YAAAAA! Just practicing some...jiu jitsu.

FLORA. Jiu jitsu? I used to drive one of those.

(**JACK** *reacts and then spots* **BARNEY**'*s disguise on the floor and rushes to retrieve it.*)

BLANCHE. (*Approaching* **BARNEY**.) What's happened to Mr. Smith? He's soaking wet.

JACK. (*Trying to get the disguise back on him.*) He's fine. He just has a little...drinking problem.

BLANCHE. (*Recognizing him.*) Oh my goodness! It's him! It's Barney.

ROSE. Barney? Barney Effward?

FLORA. Who's Barney Effward?

ROSE. What in God's name is he doing here?

JACK. (*Busily putting* **BARNEY**'*s disguise back on him.*) Ssh! Keep it down. As far as you're concerned he's not here. And he's not Barney. He's *Mr. Smith*. Okay?

BLANCHE. What are you up to, Jack? What have you done?

JACK. I haven't done anything. Nurse Ratched made me promise to keep him under wraps or she'll testify on behalf of my kids.

ROSE. Your kids?

JACK. Yeah, they're trying to have me declared incompetent.

FLORA. How awful.

ROSE. That witch!

JACK. Yeah, witch with a capital "B." Anyway, you mustn't let on that Barney's here.

ROSE. No problem. I'm not going to let on that he's here. I'm just going to kill him!

(*She raises her cane as if she's going to clock him with it, but* **JACK** *stops her.*)

JACK. Rose, Rose, calm down! We can't just kill him.

FLORA. Why not? I say we blow his brains out!

JACK. Flora!

BLANCHE. No, we can't do that. They'll know it was murder.

ROSE. We could make it look like an accident. That wouldn't be hard in this place.

FLORA. Yes, he could *accidentally* blow his brains out. I'll go and get my Glock.

> (*She turns to go.*)

ROSE. Don't be ridiculous. You don't have a Glock.

BLANCHE. Besides, how does a catatonic man accidentally shoot himself?

ROSE. I've got it. An accidental drug overdose. All we need to do is pool a few of our prescriptions together and put him to sleep. Permanently.

FLORA. Ooh, that's good. But how do we get him to swallow a bunch of pills?

ROSE. We could just put it in a glass of water and make him drink it.

BLANCHE. How do we get him to do that?

ROSE. He's catatonic, not unconscious. If you put something in his mouth, he'll swallow it.

JACK. You know something, that could actually work.

ROSE. Of course it would work! So what goodies do we have at our disposal?

> (*They all pull out their bottles of medication and line them up on the table.*)

FLORA. I've got my Aricept and my beta-blockers.

ROSE. Oh, heart medication, that's good. I've got Lipitor, Capotem, Tenex, Dibenzyline, Mannitol, Diamox, Liotrix…

FLORA. What have you got, Jack?

JACK. What more do you need?

> (*Bitterly.*)

They've locked up all my medications, ever since my "accidental overdose." All I've got on me is some bootleg Viagra.

(He holds up a Tic-Tac bottle of blue pills and shakes them. The women stare at him.)

You never know when you might need 'em.

FLORA. We can give him those for dessert!

ROSE. At least he'll die a happy man.

JACK. It gives new meaning to the term "dead stiff."

BLANCHE. Okay, that ought to be enough to do it.

JACK. You think?

BLANCHE. The only thing we have to decide now is who's going to feed him this little – cocktail.

(A beat as they consider the enormity of what he's saying.)

FLORA. I'll do it!

ROSE. Oh, I don't know, Flora. You might forget what you're doing halfway through and end up downing it yourself.

JACK. I'll do it. He's my roommate. I've got the most access to him.

ROSE. Are you sure?

JACK. I'm sure. Just give me the stuff and I'll take care of it.

BLANCHE. I'll help you.

FLORA. That's right, Blanche. Send him straight to hell!

ROSE. So when are you going to do it?

FLORA. Soon as possible, I say.

JACK. What about tonight? After Ilsa She-Wolf of the SS goes off duty.

BLANCHE. Excellent. It's a date.

HARPER. *(Offstage.)* Take a message. I'll call him back as soon as I'm finished here.

JACK. Oh-oh.

(**JACK** *proceeds to finish dressing* **BARNEY** *as the ladies whip their prescription bottles out of sight.*)

JACK. *(Cont.)* Now don't forget, you don't know this is Barney, right? He's Mr. Smith.

FLORA. Who is?

JACK. That's my girl!

(**HARPER** *enters. They all affect an air of nonchalance.*)

HARPER. So, what are you all chatting about?

(*She gives* **JACK** *a meaningful look.*)

JACK. Oh, you know. The usual. Memory loss.

ROSE. Medications.

BLANCHE. Mortality.

HARPER. Scintillating. Well I hate to interrupt, but it's time to get Mr. Smith settled in his room.

(*She starts to wheel* **BARNEY** *toward* **JACK***'s room upstage center.* **ROSE** *waves.*)

ROSE. Nice to meet you, Mr. Smith.

(**HARPER** *and* **BARNEY** *exit.*)

Right then, let's go get these pills sorted out.

BLANCHE. Wait a second. We're not really going to do this, are we?

ROSE. What, kill him? Why not? He's got it coming.

FLORA. And it's the perfect opportunity to get our revenge.

BLANCHE. You know what they say about revenge, Flora –

(**BLANCHE** *nods off.*)

ROSE. It's a dish best served cold?

JACK. It converts a little right into a great wrong?

FLORA. My money's on Rose.

BLANCHE. *(Waking up and continuing as if nothing has happened.)* – Before you go down that road, dig two graves.

FLORA. Ooh, that's a good one.

BLANCHE. Yes, my dad used to…

> *(She nods off again.)*

ROSE. And she's off again.

BLANCHE. *(Waking up again.)* – say that all the time. Anyway, I mean –

ROSE. She's back on again.

BLANCHE. – As despicable as Barney is, he hasn't actually killed anybody. If we go through with this it'll make us worse than he is.

> *(She falls asleep again.)*

JACK. It's like having a conversation with the Clapper.

> *(Singing.)*

Clap on,

> *(He claps.)*

clap off.

> *(**ROSE** and **FLORA** join in as **BLANCHE** wakes up.)*

JACK, ROSE, & FLORA. *(Singing.)* *(Melody improvised.)* The Clapper!

BLANCHE. I'm serious. We're talking about cold-blooded murder!

ROSE. You say that like it's a bad thing, Blanche.

BLANCHE. Well, think about it seriously for a moment. Could you really live with yourself having taken another human life?

ROSE. Define human.

BLANCHE. And besides, he's never going to know what hit him. How satisfying is it going to be taking revenge on a turnip?

ROSE. You've got a point there.

BLANCHE. Is it really worth spending the rest of our days in maximum security?

FLORA. Yes, those prisons smell worse than Departure Point.

JACK. And it won't be much fun if we can't make him suffer.

ROSE. True.

BLANCHE. I think we should be concentrating on saving our own lives rather than doing away with his.

ROSE. Maybe you're right. We can let the courts deal with him.

FLORA. I'm confused. So we're not killing him now?

BLANCHE. That's right, Flora.

FLORA. Pity. It was a lovely thought.

(The intercom clicks on.)

VOICE. *(Offstage.)* Chairobics class with Cheryl begins in the activity room in five minutes. Five minutes to chairobics.

(The intercom clicks off.)

ROSE. Oh no, not Cheryl – she's a slave driver.

FLORA. Which one is Cheryl?

ROSE. You know, the one with the big tits and the leg-warmers.

JACK. Really? Maybe it's time I took up chairobics.

(He starts off.)

BLANCHE. Get back here, you!

JACK. So I got a thing for leg-warmers, so sue me!

FLORA. Come on Rose. If we hurry, we might get there before the class is over.

(As they exit.)

Aren't you coming, Blanche?

BLANCHE. No, not today.

*(**ROSE** and **FLORA** exit upstage left. **JACK** turns to **BLANCHE**.)*

JACK. *(In his best gangster voice.)* Seein' as we ain't gonna grease this F-word character, you want maybe I should take you to da movies instead?

BLANCHE. That would be lovely Jack. It might take my mind off things for a while.

JACK. My thoughts exactly.

(He gives her a kiss on the cheek.)

BLANCHE. "Drinks" in your room afterwards as usual?

JACK. Not my room. I got Mr. Potato Head in there.

BLANCHE. Oh yes, of course. Maybe we should kill him after all.

JACK. Isn't your roommate off visiting her niece or something?

BLANCHE. No, that was last week.

JACK. Oh. We could have a quickie – er, quick drink – in here, as long as we're quiet.

BLANCHE. In here? What if Nurse Harper should catch us?

JACK. So what if she does? What's the worst that could happen?

BOTH. They could throw us out!

(They laugh at themselves, and then slowly the reality of what they've said dawns on them.)

JACK. *(Leading her out.)* Come on, Blanche, let's go break our dentures on some overpriced popcorn.

(Lights fade, then shift to indicate a passage of time.)

Scene III

*(Later that night. The room is dimly lit. **BARNEY**, dressed in pajamas, enters stealthily from his and **JACK**'s room. He stops just inside the common room, does a quick shoulder check to make sure the coast is clear, and dashes to the telephone by the window seat. He dials furiously.)*

BARNEY. Hello, Mortimer? It's me... Barney... Effward! ...No, this isn't a joke... Well I got better, OK? Listen, you've got to get me out of this place. They've put me in with a bunch of crazy old farts who are planning to kill me! ...I'm totally serious! I heard them talking about it earlier... The cops? I can't do that! The minute they see me walking and talking, they'll throw me back in jail! Can't you get a change of venue or whatever it's called? ...Well, make it snappy. They're planning to do it tonight! They've pooled their prescriptions and they're going to feed me some kind of cocktail...not a martini, a *drug* cocktail... How soon can you get here? Well, I'll try and survive that long. And Mortimer – can you bring me a corned beef sandwich or something? I haven't had any solid food for days. All they ever feed me is pudding!

JACK. *(Offstage.)* Come on, Blanche. It's cocktail time.

BARNEY. Cocktail time? Oh my God! They're going to do it now! I gotta go.

*(**BARNEY** hangs up. He looks around frantically, sees the window seat and decides to hide in it. He starts toward it just as **BLANCHE** and **JACK** enter upstage right. He realizes he doesn't have time to get there and instead dives to the floor and crawls to downstage of the sofa and flattens himself on the floor.)*

JACK. So, you sure you're up for this?

BLANCHE. You bet. I've been thinking about it ever since our conversation this afternoon.

JACK. You're not worried about getting caught?

BLANCHE. It's worth the risk.

JACK. That's my girl.

BLANCHE. You got the pills?

JACK. Yes indeedy.

> (*He holds up his Tic-Tac package and rattles it.* **BARNEY** *reacts with fear.*)

BLANCHE. Good. I'll be right back!

> (**BLANCHE** *crosses downstage left and exits into the bathroom.* **JACK** *crosses downstage right to the window seat to get his bottle of scotch. As this happens,* **BARNEY** *crawls around to hide upstage of the sofa. Humming happily to himself,* **JACK** *turns on the lamp on the side table downstage right, crosses to the sofa, and sits.* **BLANCHE** *re-enters with a pair of Dixie cups and crosses to join him, holding the cups out to him.*)

JACK. (*Pouring.*) How's that?

BLANCHE. Easy. A little of this stuff goes a long way.

JACK. Okay, here we go.

> (*He pops a pill, looks at the bottle for a quick moment and then pops a second one before chasing it with a shot of whisky.*)

BLANCHE. Do you really think you should be mixing those pills with alcohol?

JACK. Don't worry, I know what I'm doing.

> (**BARNEY***'s head pops up, with a look of terror. He gasps.* **BARNEY** *ducks down as* **JACK** *and* **BLANCHE** *turn to see where the noise came from.*)

BLANCHE. What was that?

JACK. Probably Mrs. Draper snoring. That woman could drown out a snowblower.

> (**JACK** *pours himself another shot.*)

I think we need a little more of this.

(He tops up her cup.)

BLANCHE. Careful. This stuff is lethal.

JACK. That's the point.

BLANCHE. Ooh, you are a bad boy.

JACK. Well, if I'm such a bad boy, what does that make you?

BLANCHE. I guess I'm just your partner in crime.

JACK. Come here.

(They toast, clink their Dixie cups, drink, and kiss.)

BLANCHE. How long does it take to work?

JACK. Don't worry, it's very quick.

BLANCHE. Then let's get to it.

(She falls asleep, her Dixie cup cradled in her arm.)

JACK. Oh no. Blanche! Blanche! Come on, sweetheart, don't quit on me now!

(She snores. He lays her head down on the sofa.)

I'm all ready to go! I'm locked and loaded! We've got to take care of this now!

(He gives her a shake. She snores. He rises in frustration.)

Well I might as well make one of us comfortable. I'll get you a blanket.

(He gets up and crosses above the sofa to his bedroom.)

(Muttering as he goes.) I just can't catch a break...

*(As he disappears, **BARNEY** crawls around and gets into the window box. **JACK** opens the door, turns on the light, and stops in his tracks.)*

What the hell? Where is he? Are you in the can, Effward?

(He goes into the room to check.)

(Offstage.) Huh. That's weird.

(He comes back into the common room.)

Blanche.

> *(He crosses quickly to the sofa and tries to wake up*
> **BLANCHE**.*)*

Hey Blanche, Effward's disappeared. His chair's there, but he's not in it. We need to find him. Blanche, honey, wake up!

> *(***BLANCHE*** *is down for the count.)*

I'd better report this or they'll blame me for it.

> *(He starts out then turns back.)*

Oops, guess I should hide the incriminating evidence.

> *(He picks up the bottle, takes it to the window seat*
> *and lifts the lid.* **BARNEY** *pops out like a Jack-in-*
> *the-Box.)*

BARNEY. Aaaaaghh!

JACK. Aaaaaghh!

BARNEY. No, please, don't do it! Don't kill me!

JACK. What? What are you doing in there?

BARNEY. Hiding from you! Please! I'll make you a deal – whatever you want!

JACK. What are you talking about? *Why* are you talking?

BARNEY. What? Oh, the catatonia. That was just an act.

JACK. So you've been compos mentis this whole time?

BARNEY. That's right.

JACK. And my conversation with the girls this afternoon, you heard all that?

BARNEY. Lipitor, Capotem, Tenex, Dibenzyline? Yeah, I heard it all – including the Viagra for dessert. But listen, you don't have to kill me.

JACK. You're right. I don't. I'm just going to call the cops.

> *(He heads for the phone.)*

BARNEY. No no no no no! Hang on a second. I've got a better idea.

JACK. Oh yeah?

BARNEY. Oh yeah. A *much* better idea.

> (*He checks to see that* **BLANCHE** *is still asleep.*)

How would you like all of your retirement money back, and then some?

JACK. Who's gonna give it to me, you?

BARNEY. Yes.

JACK. And why should I believe anything you say – especially when it comes to money?

BARNEY. Because I have a lot of it. You don't think I'd have pulled off a scam like this without having an exit strategy in place, do you?

JACK. What are you talking about, a bunch of cash in some numbered account?

BARNEY. Not cash. Something you in particular would appreciate.

JACK. What?

BARNEY. Diamonds. Ten million bucks' worth.

JACK. Ten million bucks? That's a lot of diamonds.

BARNEY. Not as many as you might think. They're D color flawless stones – about three carats a pop.

> (**JACK** *whistles in appreciation.*)

JACK. And where are they?

BARNEY. I can get my hands on them easily enough. But first I've got to get the hell out of here.

JACK. What's stopping you?

BARNEY. This –

> (*He holds up his leg to reveal a security bracelet around his ankle.*)

JACK. What's that?

BARNEY. A security bracelet. The judge wasn't taking any chances when she shipped me off to the hospital.

JACK. Can't say that I blame her. How does it work?

BARNEY. It's got a GPS in it or something. If I take so much as one step out the front door, it goes off like a fire alarm. Same thing if I try to cut it off, or tamper with it. Anything like that and the SWAT team will be here inside of four minutes. I heard the cops talking about it when they transferred me here.

(Unnoticed by JACK *and* BARNEY, BLANCHE *wakes up and overhears the following. Whenever* JACK *or* BARNEY *looks in her direction, she pretends to be asleep.)*

JACK. So what's the deal?

BARNEY. Simple. You get me out and I'll cut you in for ten percent. That's a million bucks.

JACK. Forget it.

BARNEY. You're going to turn down a million bucks? That's more than enough to keep you here for the rest of your life.

JACK. It's not just me we're talking about. There are a lot of other people here that you've ripped off. Tell you what – let's split the stones fifty-fifty and you've got a deal.

BARNEY. Fifty-fifty? Are you out of your mind??

JACK. Remember the alternative.

BARNEY. OK, thirty percent.

JACK. Fifty.

BARNEY. Thirty-five.

JACK. *(Getting up.)* That's it, I'm calling 911.

BARNEY. Alright! Fifty it is, you crook!

JACK. Said the pot to the kettle...

*(*JACK, *feeling a stirring in his loins, crosses his legs uncomfortably.* BARNEY *notices this.)*

BARNEY. What's the matter with you?

JACK. Oh, just an old injury rearing its ugly head.

BARNEY. Injury, eh? Soft tissue?

JACK. Not anymore.

(Crossing his legs with difficulty.)

JACK. *(Cont.)* So, what's your plan?

BARNEY. You find me a way out of here. Once I'm free, you get your diamonds.

JACK. You think I was born yesterday? Here's how it's going to work – you get the stones here and I appraise them. If they're as good as you say they are, we divvy them up. THEN we get you out of here.

> *(Beat.)*

BARNEY. *(Reluctantly.)* Fine. In the meantime, I'd feel a lot better if you disposed of the hemlock.

JACK. What?

> (**BARNEY** *points to the cup. The penny drops for* **JACK**.)

Oh, of course.

> (**JACK** *exits into the bathroom. We hear the sound of the toilet flushing.*)

(Offstage.) Done!

BARNEY. Thank you. Maybe now I can get some sleep.

> *(He exits into his and* **JACK**'s room. **JACK** *comes in from the bathroom, holding the Dixie cup. He checks to make sure the coast is clear, and downs the scotch inside it.)*

BLANCHE. What are you doing, Jack?

JACK. Well, you don't expect me to waste perfectly good single malt, do you?

BLANCHE. No, what are you doing making a deal with that snake?

JACK. I know how to handle this guy.

BLANCHE. Like you did when you handed him your life's savings? The man's a crook! How do you even know these diamonds exist?

JACK. It's okay. Nothing's going to happen until I get to see them for myself.

BLANCHE. And what if they're fakes?

JACK. Honey, if there's one thing I know, it's diamonds.

BLANCHE. Even if they are real, there's no way he's going to just hand over five million dollars to you.

JACK. If he doesn't, I'll just call the cops.

BLANCHE. What if you get caught? You'll be an accessory!

JACK. This is *our money* we're talking about, Blanche, and I'm going to get it back – whatever the risk.

BLANCHE. But it's a crime. You'll be breaking the law!

JACK. Look, I'm not just doing this for myself, I'm doing it for all of us.

BLANCHE. Why don't we just hand him over to the police? Tell them about the diamonds.

JACK. Sure, we could do that. And then we'll never see a dime. I know this is risky, but what's the alternative? Departure Point? Look, we've only got a few years left – this is our chance to make the best of them...

BLANCHE. We'll have to talk it over with Flora and Rose.

JACK. Absolutely.

BLANCHE. Jack, are you sure you know what you're doing?

JACK. This guy got the better of me once, Blanche. I'm not going to let it happen again.

BLANCHE. Well, we can talk about it in the morning. There's nothing more to be done tonight.

JACK. *(Squirming in his seat.)* There is *one* pressing matter...

(He looks down. She follows his gaze.)

BLANCHE. Oh. Oh dear. Well...

(She stands and begins unbuttoning her blouse.)

...we'd better do something about that, hadn't we?

*(They embrace just as the door opens and **FLORA** comes out of her room, wearing her nightie and carrying her purse. She spots **JACK** and **BLANCHE**.)*

FLORA. *(Whispering.)* Oh! I wasn't expecting to see you two here. So – are you going to do it?

*(**BLANCHE** and **JACK** look at each other.)*

BLANCHE & JACK. Do what?

FLORA. You know – kill Barney.

BLANCHE. No! We're not killing him now, Flora, remember?

FLORA. We're not? Silly me. Can't keep anything in my head these days. Oh well, nightie-night, dears.

> *(She totters back to her room.)*

JACK. Oh my God.

> *(**BLANCHE** turns to **JACK**.)*

BLANCHE. *(Provocatively.)* So, where were we?

JACK. Right here.

> *(She arranges herself on the sofa. **JACK** turns off the lamp.)*

Now don't forget; if this lasts longer than four hours, I'm going to need a doctor.

BLANCHE. *(Playfully.)* If this lasts longer than four hours, you're going to need an undertaker!

> *(They embrace as lights fade to black.)*

Scene IV

(The next morning. **BARNEY** *sits in his wheelchair at the table, wearing his watch cap and sunglasses.* **NURSE HARPER** *is sitting next to him, trying to feed him pudding. His mouth is firmly closed.* **FLORA** *is on the sofa making jewelry.* **BLANCHE** *sits next to her, knitting, and* **ROSE** *is sitting at the table playing a game on her iPad.* **JACK** *enters from the upstage left archway with a newspaper, whistling happily. He crosses jauntily to the armchair downstage right, sits.)*

HARPER. You're very chipper this morning, Mr. Newman.

(He and **BLANCHE** *exchange a smile and a wink.)*

JACK. It always cheers me up to read the obituaries.

HARPER. What's cheerful about that?

JACK. Finding out I'm not in them.

(He snaps open his paper and begins to read. **HARPER** *turns back to* **BARNEY**.*)*

HARPER. Come on Mr. Smith, open sesame!

*(***BARNEY** *doesn't move.)*

One more bite of pudding, you can do it.

(Nothing.)

Here comes the choo-choo train, heading for the tunnel…

(The "tunnel" remains firmly closed.)

JACK. *(From behind his paper.)* Oh my God…

HARPER. *(Through gritted teeth.)* I haven't got all day.

(Still no response. She checks over her shoulder to make sure nobody is looking and pinches **BARNEY**'*s nose closed so he is forced to open his mouth. She shoves in the spoonful of pudding.)*

There.

(She lets go. **BARNEY** *opens his mouth and the pudding falls out.)*

HARPER. *(Cont.)* Oh for heaven's sake, now look what you've done.

> *(She slams the spoon down, picks up a napkin, dabs him with it, takes the breakfast tray, and begins to exit upstage left, muttering all the while.)*

(Muttering.) I don't know why I bother. This isn't my job. We're not a hospital. I'm doing this out of the goodness of my heart. And do I get any thanks for my efforts? No...

> *(As she exits,* **JACK** *leaps up and follows her to the archway.)*

JACK. The coast is clear. Quick, before she gets back.

> *(***BARNEY*** *removes his sunglasses. The others immediately drop what they are doing and join* **ROSE** *at the table.)*

(Coming back to join the others.) Now where were we?

ROSE. *(Typing furiously.)* We're just about done, actually. All I need now, Barney, is your customer number.

BARNEY. *(Very quickly.)* FL34005990391880205QV7

FLORA. My goodness. How could you possibly remember all that?

BARNEY. You'd be surprised what ten million bucks can do for your memory.

ROSE. Got it. Now what's your password?

BARNEY. Shystermeister1.

JACK. How apt.

ROSE. Recipient's name... Mr. Jack Newman.

BARNEY. Jack Newman?

JACK. Well, we can't very well ship them to Mr. Smith, can we?

ROSE. *(Typing.)* Jack... Newman...

JACK. Heads up – Harper's back!

(BARNEY puts on his sunglasses and slumps back, while the others scurry to their original positions and adopt an air of nonchalance as HARPER enters upstage left, crosses to the closet downstage left, gets a big bag of Depends, closes the door, and exits. Throughout this, we hear the following:)

HARPER. *(Muttering.)* Nobody notices anyway. I mean it's not as if I'm ever going to get a promotion or anything in this godforsaken place, let alone a raise. What am I doing now? Changing diapers.

(Calling, as she exits upstage right.)

Cross your legs, Mrs. Draper, I'm on my way.

(She disappears.)

JACK. It's a wonder she's single, isn't it?

(They all gather around the table again. BARNEY removes his sunglasses.)

ROSE. And...

(ROSE taps a key with satisfaction.)

...we're done. The diamonds will be here by eleven-thirty tomorrow morning, guaranteed.

BLANCHE. Assuming they really are diamonds.

BARNEY. You'll see when they get here.

FLORA. I can't believe it. Tomorrow we'll all have our savings back!

BLANCHE. I'm really not comfortable with this.

JACK. What's the problem? I check the stones, make sure they're worth what he says they are, and *if* I'm satisfied, we get our cut.

BLANCHE. But we're letting him get away with five million dollars of other people's money!

ROSE. That's true. What about all those other people he's ripped off?

BARNEY. Oh quit your complaining. You're getting yours back, aren't you? I don't see the problem.

BLANCHE. That's because you're a crook! Don't you care at all about your victims?

BARNEY. Victims. Pfft. The only thing they were victims of is their own greed. As far as I'm concerned, anyone who's stupid enough to believe they can make a thirty percent return on their investment year after year deserves exactly what they get.

ROSE. Just a minute here –

BARNEY. Look, it's like the old saying – if something seems too good to be true, it probably is.

(Beat. They are all somewhat gobsmacked.)

FLORA. I just have one question.

JACK. What is it, Flora?

FLORA. *(Pointing at BARNEY.)* When do we shoot him?

BARNEY. *(To JACK.)* I thought you said you'd called off the dogs?

ROSE. Flora, dear, you remember, we're not killing him anymore.

FLORA. We're not? Oh, right.

(The intercom suddenly sputters into action.)

VOICE. *(Offstage.)* Ladies and gentlemen, the Walmart shuttle will be leaving from the front door in ten minutes. Ten minutes to the Walmart shuttle. Have fun, shoppers!

(There is a flurry of activity as ROSE, BLANCHE, and FLORA all leap to their feet and exit to their various bedrooms.)

ROSE. Oh goody. Walmart!

FLORA. Perfect timing, I'm all out of rhinestones!

BLANCHE. See you on the bus, girls.

FLORA. Won't be a moment. My teeth just need some Polyfilla.

JACK. What?

ROSE. Grip, dear. Poly-grip.

FLORA. Right, right.

ROSE. You must remind me to pick up a couple of memory sticks.

(They go.)

JACK. I don't believe it. They've just found out they're going to be millionaires and where's the first place they go? Walmart.

(He gets up to leave.)

BARNEY. Where are you going?

JACK. Just getting a coffee.

BARNEY. Can you grab me a sandwich or something? I'm starving.

JACK. What's it worth to you?

BARNEY. Forget it.

JACK. Have it your way.

(He exits upstage left.)

*(***BARNEY*** gets up and stretches, jumps up and down, twists his back. As he hears the following he races back into this chair, puts on his sunglasses, and slumps.)*

HARPER. *(Offstage.)* I assure you, Mr. Mortimer, his condition hasn't changed, but if you insist…

MORTIMER. *(Offstage.)* I'd like to see that for myself, if you don't mind.

(They enter upstage right.)

HARPER. There he is! Just as I told you.

MORTIMER. What's with the outfit? He looks like a burglar.

HARPER. If the shoe fits…

MORTIMER. Now now, Nurse Harper, none of the charges against my client has been proven in court.

*(Crossing to ***BARNEY*** and removing the sunglasses.)*

Hmm.

> *(Loudly.)*

MORTIMER. *(Cont.)* Hello, Barney!

> *(No response. He waves his hand in front of* **BARNEY**'s *face.)*

It's me, Mortimer!

> *(Even louder.)*

CAN YOU HEAR ME?

> *(He turns to* **HARPER**. **BARNEY** *winces.)*

HARPER. He's catatonic, Mr. Mortimer. He's not deaf.

MORTIMER. *(Holding up a brown paper bag.)* I brought your sandwich! Fresh from Schwartz's.

> *(He turns to* **HARPER** *with a sigh.* **BARNEY** *stares longingly at the sandwich, trying not to drool.)*

I don't understand. I spoke to him on the phone last night. He was talking perfectly normally.

> *(***JACK** *starts to enter upstage left, holding a cup of coffee. He sees a stranger in the room and retreats slightly, eavesdropping.)*

He told me someone was going to kill him.

HARPER. I don't see how that's possible.

MORTIMER. Be that as it may, my primary concern is for the safety of my client. I think the prudent thing to do is to have him moved to another location as soon as possible.

HARPER. You'll have to speak with Dr. Anderson about that.

> *(***HARPER** *crosses toward the exit upstage right.* **MORTIMER** *follows.)*

He's in a meeting at the moment. If you'd like to come with me, I'll find out when he's free.

MORTIMER. I don't have much time. I have to be in court in half an hour.

HARPER. The doctor is a very busy man, Mr. Mortimer, but I'll see what I can do.

(They exit upstage right. **BARNEY** *tears into the sandwich as* **JACK** *steps into the room.)*

BARNEY. Oh, thank God. Solid food at last.

(Mouth full.)

Mmm. Oh, is that ever good.

*(***BARNEY*** *continues to eat under the following.)*

JACK. You called your lawyer? What were you thinking?

BARNEY. You were plotting to kill me! I had to do something to save my butt.

JACK. Well congratulations, you saved it! Enjoy your new digs!

BARNEY. Jack! You gotta do something! You can't let them ship me out of here!

JACK. Why not?

BARNEY. Why not? Those diamonds are going to be arriving here tomorrow and I won't be here to receive them!

JACK. Not my problem.

BARNEY. Those are my diamonds.

JACK. Oh no they're not. That package is addressed to me. They're *my* diamonds.

BARNEY. And how are you going to explain ten million dollars worth of diamonds suddenly falling into your lap?

JACK. Who am I going to have to explain it to? Who's going to know?

BARNEY. My lawyer, for one. All I have to do is spill the beans about our little scheme here and he'll leak it to the cops. You'll end up in the dock right beside me. You and all your girlfriends.

(A beat as **JACK** *ponders the implications of this.)*

Like it or not, we're stuck with each other, buddy. So you'd better make sure they don't ship me out of here.

JACK. *(Pointing at the sandwich.)* You gonna eat the rest of that?

BARNEY. Damn right I am.

> *(He polishes off the other half.* **BLANCHE** *enters from her room in her coat and hat, looking very stylish.)*

BLANCHE. Are you coming shopping with us, Jack?

JACK. *(Putting down his cup.)* No, I've – got a few things to take care of here. Have fun!

> *(She exits upstage right with a wave.* **ROSE** *and* **FLORA** *enter from their room, wearing coats and hats. There is a shopping basket attached to the front of* **ROSE**'s *walker.)*

FLORA. What was it I was supposed to remind you to get?

ROSE. Memory sticks, dear.

FLORA. Oh yes, memory sticks!

> *(They exit upstage right.* **BARNEY** *and* **JACK** *watch them go.)*

BARNEY. Adorable, aren't they? Mind you, they won't look quite so adorable in orange jumpsuits.

JACK. You wouldn't.

BARNEY. In a heartbeat. So just find a way to keep me here, and we'll all live happily ever after.

MORTIMER. *(Offstage.)* Tell him to cover for me – this is taking longer than I thought.

> *(***JACK*** *looks around in a panic and races into the closet.)*

(Entering, talking on his phone.) I can't wait to get out of here. I hate these places, they're nothing but germ factories.

> *(He closes his phone, thinks for a second, opens it again. He pulls a small bottle of hand-sanitizer spray from his pocket, sprays his phone, wipes it clean with a hanky, and crosses to the table. He sets down his briefcase and pulls out a file.* **JACK** *enters wearing a white coat and stethoscope. He*

slams the door behind him, startling **MORTIMER.**
He crosses toward **BARNEY.***)*

JACK. Ah, Mr. Smith! How are we feeling today?

(He listens to **BARNEY***'s chest with the stethoscope, looks in his ears, making a great show of examining him. In the midst of this he "notices"* **MORTIMER.***)*

Oh. And who might you be?

MORTIMER. I'm Alfred Mortimer, Mr. – Smith's lawyer.

JACK. Nice to meet you. I'm Dr. Anderson.

MORTIMER. You're Dr. Anderson?

JACK. Indeed.

MORTIMER. *(Confused, looking upstage right to where he just came from.)* I thought you were in a meeting.

JACK. Meeting? Oh, I hate meetings. Avoid them whenever I can.

MORTIMER. I'm glad you're here. You look familiar. Have we met?

JACK. I don't think so.

MORTIMER. Funny. I never forget a face.

(Looking at **JACK** *closely.)*

I've got it – that guy on TV. You know, the one with the annoying commercials. The Jack of Diamonds.

JACK. Yeah, I get that all the time. But no, that's not me. I'm much better looking. Heh, heh, heh!

(No response from **MORTIMER.***)*

So, how can I help?

MORTIMER. I'm concerned about my client. Last night I received a very troubling phone call from Mr. Smith here. He claimed there were people in this institution who were planning to murder him.

JACK. *(Laughing.)* Oh, that's ridiculous! Look at him – the man's clearly in no condition to make phone calls. He's completely unresponsive. I'll show you –

(JACK slaps BARNEY across the face a couple of times. BARNEY doesn't respond. MORTIMER turns away to open his briefcase. BARNEY slaps JACK's cheeks and they scuffle.)

MORTIMER. Be that as it may, I think it's best that I err on the side of caution here. I took the liberty of obtaining a court order this morning to move Mr. Smith to another facility.

(He turns back to them, holding a piece of paper.)

JACK. Another facility? I'm afraid that's impossible. He's in no condition to be moved.

MORTIMER. Why not? He seems fine to me – well, apart from the obvious.

JACK. Oh, he's a very sick man.

MORTIMER. Don't worry, the doctors there will take care of him. Now, if I could just have you sign off on this, we can have him out of here right now.

(BARNEY, terrified, lets out a yelp.)

(Jumps.) What was that?

JACK. That was Mr. Smith.

MORTIMER. He barked.

JACK. I know. He's suffering from a very rare infection – canine strepto-klepto-coccus.

MORTIMER. Sounds serious.

(BARNEY, in a state of panic, begins to hyperventilate.)

JACK. It is.

MORTIMER. I see. What are the symptoms?

JACK. Well, as you can see, there are many.

(With a look to BARNEY.)

Rapid, shallow breathing.

(BARNEY sticks his tongue out and pants like a dog, indicating his forehead with his eyes. JACK

takes the cue and wipes **BARNEY**'s *forehead with a hanky.*)

Profuse sweating.

(**BARNEY** *slumps over to one side.*)

(*Taking his cue.*) Loss of balance…

(**JACK** *shoves him into a vertical position.* **BARNEY** *slumps over to the other side.* **JACK** *sets him straight.*)

(*Warming to the task.*) And as you just heard, a tendency to make this odd barking sound, like a bloodhound.

(**BARNEY** *obliges with a tinny, high-pitched bark.*)

MORTIMER. That sounds more like a chihuahua.

(**BARNEY** *adjusts his bark accordingly, producing a more bloodhound-like howl.*)

JACK. Mr. Mortimer, this disease is my specialty. Believe me, moving him would be very dangerous.

MORTIMER. But he's in danger as it is! The person who called me last night identified himself as Barney and said someone was going to kill him!

JACK. Impossible. Look at him.

(**BARNEY** *howls again.*)

Let's face it, Mr. Mortimer. There are a lot of people out there who would like to get their revenge on Mr. – Smith. I'm sure it was just a prank call.

MORTIMER. Possibly.

JACK. He'll be much safer where he is. Trust me, he's in very good hands.

(**JACK** *turns to* **BARNEY** *and smiles.* **BARNEY** *glares in response, then howls once more.*)

Good dog.

(*He pats* **BARNEY** *on the head.* **BARNEY** *growls.*)

Bad dog.

MORTIMER. You may be right, Doctor, but my client's safety is my primary concern. I still think it would be best if we have him moved. So, if you could just sign the papers, I'll go and collect his things.

> *(He crosses toward* **BARNEY** *as if to wheel him away.)*

JACK. STOP!

> *(***MORTIMER** *leaps away.)*

MORTIMER. What is it?

JACK. He can't be moved.

MORTIMER. Why?

JACK. Canine strepto-klepto-coccus is highly contagious.

MORTIMER. It is?

JACK. Yes, and it has a very high mortality rate.

MORTIMER. Mortality rate?

JACK. Oh yes, the life expectancy is usually no more than... twenty minutes.

MORTIMER. Twenty minutes?

> *(Checking his watch.)*

Ah...well, umm, I tell you what, I-I-I I'll have to make a few phone calls and I'll get right back to you.

> *(He puts the paper back in his briefcase, pulls out his bottle of hand sanitizer, and sprays his hands and face with it. As an afterthought he sprays his briefcase while he's at it.)*

I trust you'll call me if his condition changes?

JACK. Don't worry, you'll be the first to know.

MORTIMER. *(Running toward the exit.)* Thank you for your time, Doctor. I'll be in touch.

> *(He bolts out upstage right, spraying the air around him as he goes.)*

BARNEY. Canine strepto-klepto-coccus?

JACK. You're the one who barked. Anyway, it worked, didn't it?

BARNEY. For now.

JACK. I'd better get rid of this outfit before the real Dr. Anderson shows up.

(He exits into the closet. HARPER enters from upstage right and sees BARNEY sitting alone.)

HARPER. Dr. Anderson should be available in – where did he go?

(Opening the door to BARNEY's room.)

Mr. Mortimer?

(Looking around, seeing no sign of him.)

How odd. Well, we can't be leaving you out here all alone, now can we?

(She wheels BARNEY into his room just as JACK comes in from the closet, minus the doctor's jacket and stethoscope. HARPER closes the bedroom door.)

JACK. Good. She can deal with him for a while. I need some air.

(He exits upstage right. HARPER comes out of the bedroom.)

HARPER. *(Into the bedroom.)* I'll come and collect you in a little while, Mr. Smith.

(Muttering to herself as she crosses to the exit upstage left.)

Now – where did that Mr. Newman get to? He's supposed to be looking after him. I should have known better than to trust a TV pitchman...

(Mimicking JACK's commercial.)

"Have I Got a Deal for You!"

(...And she's gone. A beat. FLORA re-enters from upstage right. She comes into the room and pauses, slightly confused.)

FLORA. Now, what did I come back for?

> *(She opens her purse and peers in.)*

Oh yes, that's right.

> *(Facing downstage she pulls out a small Glock, quickly pushes opens* **BARNEY**'*s bedroom door and, doing her best SWAT impression, points her gun into the room and fires.)*
>
> *(blackout)*

End of Act I

ACT II

Scene I

*(The following morning. There is yellow crime-scene tape over **JACK** and **BARNEY**'s door. All the residents, except **BARNEY**, are in the room. **JACK** is pacing. **FLORA** is sitting on the window seat working on her jewelry.)*

JACK. Where the hell is that UPS guy?

(Looking at his watch.)

They said eleven-thirty, guaranteed.

BLANCHE. I'll be glad to see the back of those policemen. I've never felt so violated in my life – pawing through my lingerie like that...they were so rude!

FLORA. Oh, I thought the tall one was very nice.

BLANCHE. Asking the same questions over and over again, treating us like common criminals!

ROSE. Yes, and forcing us to sit out here until all hours while they tore our rooms apart.

BLANCHE. By the time I got to bed I was so upset I couldn't sleep a wink.

JACK. At least you got to bed. I had to spend the night camped out here on the couch.

FLORA. I couldn't sleep either. So I decided to put the time to good use. Look.

(She shows off her bracelet.)

ROSE. Ooh, that's a lovely bracelet, Flora.

FLORA. That's just what that nice tall policeman said. He liked it so much he wanted me to make one for his wife.

ROSE. That stone in the middle is interesting. What is it?

JACK. *(Peering at it.)* Hmm. Looks like a piece of hematite.

FLORA. You could be right, Jack. I have no idea. I just picked it up somewhere.

> *(**NURSE HARPER** enters from upstage right wheeling **BARNEY**, who is in his disguise.)*

HARPER. Here we are, Mr. Smith, back with all your friends.

JACK. *(To **HARPER**.)* So?

HARPER. According to the police the bullet went right through the back of Mr. Smith's wheelchair, which is a mystery because if he was sitting in it, he should have a hole in him right about here.

> *(She jabs **BARNEY** in the chest with her finger.)*

JACK. Where's the bullet?

HARPER. There's no sign of it. It's not in the room and they couldn't find anything on the x-rays.

JACK. I can't understand why you gave him an x-ray to begin with.

HARPER. They thought he might have swallowed it.

ROSE. Why on earth would he do that?

HARPER. Well, it had to go somewhere. Their best guess is that the shooter took it with him. Along with his gun, of course.

JACK. So what happens now?

HARPER. *(Indicating **JACK**'s room.)* For the time being we're going to have to keep you all in lockdown. Oh, and Mr. Newman, I'm afraid you and Mr. Smith won't have access to your room for a while. It's still considered a crime scene.

> *(She exits upstage right.)*

JACK. Terrific.

> *(**BARNEY** gets up and crosses toward the phone.)*

What are you doing?

BARNEY. I'm calling my lawyer. Those stones should be here any minute. Once I've got my half I'm out of here. I'm not hanging around waiting for one of you to take another pot shot at me.

(*He begins to dial.*)

JACK. (*Taking the phone from him and hanging it up.*) Look, I've told you, it wasn't us. Nobody here is trying to kill you!

BARNEY. You could have fooled me. If it wasn't for my cranky prostate, I'd have a hole in me right about here –

(*He points to his sternum.*)

To match this one!

(*He pokes his finger through the bullet hole in the back of his wheelchair.*)

JACK. You heard Nurse Harper; whoever shot at you has left the building.

BARNEY. You don't know that for sure.

JACK. They've been through this place with a fine-toothed comb. If the shooter was still here they would have found the gun.

FLORA. Gun?

(*She reaches into her cleavage, pulls the Glock out.*)

Is this what you're looking for?

(*She waves the gun around. They all gasp and duck out of the way.*)

BARNEY. It was her! I told you one of you was trying to kill me!

FLORA. I'm sorry, who are you again?

ROSE. Oh dear, this is Barney Effward, remember?

FLORA. Oh, yes, of course.

(*Tapping her temple with the gun.*)

FLORA. *(Cont.)* Now I remember. We're supposed to blow your brains out!

> *(She takes aim. **BARNEY** dives for cover.)*

JACK. *(Taking the gun from her gently.)* No, Flora. We decided not to do that, remember?

FLORA. We did?

BLANCHE. Barney's going to make us rich instead.

FLORA. Rich?

JACK. Yes, with diamonds!

FLORA. Oh, Jack of Diamonds, right!

> *(Imitating **JACK**'s tag line.)*

Have I got a deal for *you*!!

BARNEY. I gotta say Flora, for someone who can't remember what day it is, you covered your tracks like a pro. What did you do with the bullet?

FLORA. Bullet? Ohh, of course!

> *(She indicates the stone in her new bracelet.)*

That's where I picked this up.

HARPER. *(Offstage.)* Mr. Newman?

> *(**BARNEY** scampers into his chair and puts on his glasses. **JACK** shoves the gun into his pocket. **HARPER** enters from upstage right carrying a UPS package. All take on an air of innocence.)*

Mr. Newman.

JACK. *(Snapping to attention.)* Jawold!

HARPER. I have a package here for you.

JACK. Thank you.

FLORA. Are those the diamonds?

> *(Everyone freezes.)*

HARPER. Diamonds?

FLORA. *(Repeating the gesture from **JACK**'s commercials.)* Have I got a deal for *you*!

JACK. Oh, don't mind Flora, Nurse Harpy. Harper. She's been going on all morning about my old commercials. You know, the Jack of Diamonds?

HARPER. *(Trying – and failing – to mask her distaste.)* Oh. Yes. *Those.* Lunch will be a little late today. The kitchen staff are still cleaning the fingerprint powder off the counter tops.

> *(She exits, mumbling, through the archway upstage left.* **JACK** *races over to the table downstage left with his parcel, tearing it open. The others quickly gather around. He pulls some paperwork out of the envelope.)*

JACK. These must be the appraisals.

> *(Giving them a cursory glance to confirm this.)*

Blanche honey, can you hang onto these for me?

BLANCHE. Of course, Jack.

JACK. OK, this is it – the moment of truth…

> *(He pulls a pair of glasses out of his breast pocket and puts them on. He then reaches into the envelope and fishes out a small box. He opens the lid to reveal twenty very sparkly-looking diamonds. There is a collective gasp from the others.)*

Good Lord…

BLANCHE. My goodness!

> *(He puts all but one of the stones back in the box, then pulls out his small bag of jeweller's tools.)*

Those can't be real…

> *(He puts everything on the table, pulls out his loupe and a gemstone holder, and examines the stone closely.)*

FLORA. Imagine what I could do with those.

ROSE. *(With her nose buried in the box of diamonds.)* Let me have a look.

> *(She reaches into the box.)*

JACK. *(Still examining them.)* Not yet.

BARNEY. So, Mr. Have-I-Got-A-Deal-For-You, have we got a deal?

JACK. *(Looking up, very serious.)* I've never seen anything like this in my life. If they're all like this –

> *(Doing a little jig.)*

We've hit the jackpot!

> *(They all sing and dance in celebration. As they celebrate, **FLORA** knocks **JACK**'s arm and sends the diamond flying.)*

Aaaghh! Flora! For crying out loud!

> *(He starts searching for it.)*

BLANCHE. What happened?

JACK. She knocked the stone out of my hand.

BLANCHE. Oh my goodness! We've got to find it.

> *(They all start searching on the floor, around the furniture, etc.)*

BARNEY. Damn right. Or that half a million bucks'll be coming out of your share.

ROSE. You mean that one little stone is worth half a million dollars?

JACK. At least. So for God's sake, find it!

> *(**HARPER** enters from upstage left, carrying a tray. She stops short as she sees them all crawling around. **BARNEY** puts on his glasses and slumps back in his wheelchair.)*

HARPER. What on earth are you all doing?

ROSE. *(Finding the stone.)* I've got it, I've got it!

HARPER. Got what?

JACK. *(Covering.)* The spirit of the Lord! Praise be to God!

JACK, FLORA, BLANCHE. Hallelujah! Hallelujah! Hallelujah!

> *(They struggle to their feet. **ROSE** pants as she tries valiantly to get up.)*

JACK. Need a hand there, Rose?

ROSE. What I need is a hip replacement.

(She makes it to her feet.)

HARPER. *(Setting the tray down.)* Well, Mr. Smith, it's time for lunch.

ROSE. Oh good, I'm starving.

HARPER. Not for you, I'm afraid. They're still cleaning up in the kitchen. This whole police investigation has thrown off our entire schedule. I really should be in there supervising but someone has to feed this poor soul.

JACK. I can do that for you.

HARPER. Thank you, Mr. Newman, I'm glad to see you're helping for a change.

JACK. What's on the menu?

HARPER. *(To BARNEY.)* Consommé to start, followed by puréed spinach, creamed corn and for dessert, some delicious banana pudding.

(They all pull faces of disgust except FLORA.)

FLORA. Sounds yummy.

JACK. *(Under his breath.)* If you're six months old.

(Picking up the spoon and offering BARNEY some soup.)

Okay, Mr. Smith, here comes the choo-choo train!

(BARNEY grits his teeth for a moment before allowing the choo-choo train to enter.)

HARPER. You see how well things go when everyone is willing to cooperate? Now, I'll go see about getting the rest of us fed.

(She begins to exit upstage left.)

(Muttering.) Maybe I'll get out of here before midnight after all. Not that it matters, it's not as if I have a life or anything…

(She's gone. JACK *offers* BARNEY *another spoonful.)*

JACK. *(Imitating train noises.)* Woo-woo, chugachuga chugachuga –

BARNEY. *(Pushing the spoon away.)* Get that slop away from me. Now gimme my stones.

JACK. Hold your horses. We've got to divvy them up fairly. I have to figure out what each of these is worth.

BLANCHE. How do we do that?

JACK. Each appraisal is matched up to a diamond by its serial number.

ROSE. Those tiny stones have serial numbers on them?

JACK. Yeah, they etch them on with lasers.

(Pulling his glasses out of his pocket again, he goes to the table and picks up the appraisals. Throughout the following, JACK *begins to match up the stones with the appraisals.)*

BARNEY. Well, hurry up, we've still got to figure out how to get this bracelet off my ankle.

JACK. Blanche, do me a favor, keep an eye out for The Wicked Witch of the West, will you?

BLANCHE. Of course.

(She takes a chair upstage left and sits.)

FLORA. *(Going toward* BARNEY.*)* You've got an ankle bracelet?

BARNEY. You keep your distance!

FLORA. I just wanted to have a peek. I have a lot of experience with bracelets, you know.

ROSE. It's not that kind of bracelet, Flora, dear. It's a security device, used for tracking people under house arrest. It sends out an RF signal so that the person wearing it can be located via GPS. If they stray out of a given area an alarm goes off to notify the authorities.

BARNEY. *(Impressed.)* Wow.

ROSE. They're also pretty tamper-proof. If you try to cut them off or disrupt the power supply it sets off the alarm.

BARNEY. Jeez, you sound like the damn instruction manual. Where'd you pick all that up?

ROSE. *(Pointing to her iPad.)* Google.

BARNEY. Oh. Well if you can do that, then why don't you Google me a way out of this thing?

ROSE. I'm way ahead of you.

> *(She plunks a couple of keys on her iPad.* **BLANCHE***, meanwhile, has nodded off.)*

I'm on an anarchist website here called publicenemeez dot com. They've got everything on here, from rigging electronic voting machines to making dirty bombs.

BARNEY. And here I thought you people spent all your time knitting and playing bingo.

ROSE. Ah. Here's what we need…oh, this is a piece of cake. It says here that to gain control of the unit, all we have to do is hijack the RF signal to the GPS satellite. Then we can send the command to turn the alarm off.

BARNEY. *(Impressed.)* Whatever you say, Mr. Gates. How do we do that?

ROSE. All you need is the right app.

> *(She holds up her iPad.)*

BARNEY. *(Bowled over.)* Jeez, what do you do, freelance for the CIA?

ROSE. Not anymore. Roll up your pant leg.

> *(He does so and sticks his leg up in the air, exposing the bracelet.)*

Good. Now all we have to do is tap in this access code…

> *(She taps a series of numbers and letters.)*

and…

> *(Aiming at the bracelet.)*

Enter. There, that puts us in control. Now we can tell it to do whatever we want.

BARNEY. OK?

ROSE. By typing in the appropriate command, like…

> *(Typing.)*

disarm, then…

> *(Aiming at the bracelet.)*

Enter.

> *(She hits the button. The alarm beeps. Lights flash on the bracelet. Everybody reacts with total panic except* BLANCHE, *who sleeps through it all.* JACK *rises from the table and rushes to* BARNEY *in a futile attempt to turn off the alarm.)*

BARNEY. What the hell?

JACK. Rose! What did you do?

> (ROSE *is frantically typing in "disarm" over and over, checking back on the iPad.)*

BARNEY. Oh hell, the cops'll be here in less than four minutes.

FLORA. What are we going to do? What are we going to do?

JACK. Get that iPad out of here, Rose.

ROSE. *(Holding up the iPad.)* Right. I'd better clear the history on my browser, too. Come on, Flora, let's hotfoot it out of here.

FLORA. *(Starting out.)* Exciting, isn't it?

> *(They exit into their room as fast as they can, which isn't that fast.* BLANCHE *sleeps on.)*

JACK. Come on. Do your turnip act.

> (BARNEY *puts on his glasses and assumes the position.* JACK *turns to pick up the bowl of soup.* BARNEY *realizes that the diamonds have been left in full view on the table.)*

BARNEY. The diamonds!

(**HARPER** *enters from upstage left.*)

HARPER. Lunch is ready, at long –

(*Stopping.*)

What is that racket?

JACK. *(Indicating* **BARNEY.***)* It's coming from him. I think his ankle bracelet went off.

> (**HARPER** *turns to check on* **BARNEY.** **JACK** *takes the opportunity to scoop the diamonds into his hands. He fumbles slightly, dropping one or two on the floor. He kneels down and frantically picks up the loose stone[s].*)

HARPER. *(Checking the bracelet.)* What next?

(*To* **BARNEY.***)*

I told Dr. Anderson you shouldn't be in a place like this.

(*To* **JACK.***)*

So what set this thing off anyway?

JACK. *(Still scrambling around.)* I've no idea. It suddenly started beeping.

HARPER. *(Rising.)* Not my problem. I'll let the police sort it out.

> (*She turns to* **JACK** *and discovers him on his knees with his hands clasped in front of him. He smiles nervously.*)

What are you doing?

JACK. *(Quickly glancing down and then back to her.)* Saying grace.

HARPER. *(Suspiciously.)* Really. You've been born again, have you?

JACK. Amen, Sister.

> (*She spots the appraisals on the table and takes a step toward them.*)

HARPER. What's all this paperwork here?

JACK. Umm, ah, er…

(HARPER reaches for one of the appraisals. In an effort to stop her, BARNEY howls, doubles over, and falls to the floor at the foot of his wheelchair. HARPER drops the paper and whips around to look at him. BLANCHE wakes up.)

HARPER. Oh my goodness!

(To JACK.)

Mr. Newman, come and give me a hand.

(JACK is frozen with indecision, the diamonds still clutched between his hands.)

What are you waiting for?

JACK. Uh…

(Looking skyward.)

Oh Lord, please help our brother…Smith.

HARPER. Mr. Newman, give me some help for heaven's sake!

(She grabs JACK's elbow to steer him toward BARNEY.)

Now!

(Desperately, JACK wrenches his arm away and fakes a loud sneeze.)

JACK. ACHOOO!

(As he does this, he bends forward over BARNEY's lunch tray and dumps the diamonds into the pudding [for reasons that will shortly become obvious, this bit of business should be mimed].)

HARPER. Gesundheit.

(She turns back to BARNEY. JACK takes a step toward HARPER, looks back at the pudding, and hastily picks up the spoon and stirs the diamonds into it. He crosses to help HARPER put BARNEY back in his wheelchair.)

Easy now.

JACK. Upsy daisy. There we go. All set.

> *(JACK turns, spots the appraisals, quickly collects them up, and stuffs them down his pants.)*

HARPER. *(Still fussing with* **BARNEY**.*)* My goodness. What a state of affairs. I'll have to tell Dr. Anderson about this. I think he's in the lunchroom.

> *(She turns, spots the tray.)*

Hmm. Didn't do a very good job of feeding him, did you?

> *(Picking up the tray.)*

I'll drop this off while I'm at it.

> *(She begins to exit upstage left.* **JACK** *and* **BARNEY** *look at one another, frozen with panic. As* **HARPER** *passes,* **BLANCHE** *leaps to her feet and clocks* **HARPER** *over the head with her purse.* **HARPER** *stops and turns to face downstage.)*

(To **BLANCHE**.*)* Could you hold this, please?

> *(She passes the tray to* **BLANCHE** *and promptly passes out.* **JACK** *and* **BARNEY** *race up to* **BLANCHE**.*)*

JACK. There's my girl! Way to go!

BARNEY. Yeah, quick thinking! I thought you were asleep!

JACK. *(Indicating the purse.)* Geez, what have you got in that thing, lead weights?

BLANCHE. It's all in the wrist.

BARNEY. *(Taking the tray from her.)* Allow me. We've got to get those stones back. Did you really have to toss them into the pudding?

JACK. What else was I gonna do?

BARNEY. Well get them out of there before she wakes up and carts them away.

> *(We hear the sound of a police siren approaching from the distance.)*

JACK. The cops! Quick – back in the wheelchair!

>(*JACK takes the tray from* **BARNEY** *and sets it back on the table.* **BARNEY** *sits back down, puts his glasses back on, and slumps in the wheelchair.*)

(*To* **BLANCHE**.) Blanche honey, can you get rid of Florence Nightingale here?

BLANCHE. What should I do with her?

JACK. (*Looking around frantically.*) Closet.

BLANCHE. Right.

>(*She begins to drag* **HARPER** *toward the closet. The siren, which is now very close, shuts off.*)

JACK. Uh-oh. They're here.

>(*JACK races over to the table, grabs the soup from the tray, and dumps it on* **BARNEY**'s *leg.*)

BARNEY. Hey! What the hell are you doing!

JACK. Trust me.

>(*JACK turns toward the closet and sees* **BLANCHE** *has fallen asleep beside* **HARPER** *on the floor near the closet door.*)

Oh my God.

>(*He races over to* **BLANCHE** *and tries to wake her up.*)

Blanche! Wake up!

>(*He shakes her a bit. She turns and, still asleep, cuddles up to* **HARPER**.)

BARNEY. What are we going to do?

JACK. I'll think of something.

>(*He gets an idea and exits into the closet. As he does so, a* **POLICEMAN** *enters upstage right.*)

POLICEMAN. (*Into his walkie talkie.*) All units. I've located the room where the alarm has been activated. Secure the perimeter. I'm going in.

>(*He spots the two women on the floor.*)

What the hell?

*(As he begins to cross toward them, **JACK** comes out of the closet, once again dressed in white lab coat, stethoscope, surgical mask, etc. and steps over the bodies to intercept him.)*

JACK. *(Thrusting out a hand.)* Officer? Dr. Anderson, chief administrator. How do you do?

POLICEMAN. *(Automatically shaking hands.)* Uh, fine, thanks.

*(Pointing to the sleeping **BLANCHE** and **HARPER**.)*

I'm not sure I can say the same for those two, though.

JACK. Who?

(Feigning seeing them for the first time.)

Oh, you mean them!

POLICEMAN. Are they okay? They look like they might be… dead.

JACK. Oh no, they're not dead. Not yet.

*(On hearing this, **BARNEY** takes to **JACK**, then quickly resumes his slump before the cop sees him.)*

POLICEMAN. What do you mean?

JACK. Oh, you know.

(He whispers ominously.)

They've got "it."

POLICEMAN. It?

JACK. The *disease.*

POLICEMAN. Disease? Hadn't we better check their vitals?

*(He steps toward the women and **JACK** holds up a hand to stop him.)*

JACK. No! Stop right there!

POLICEMAN. What is it?

JACK. Don't come any closer. They may still be contagious.

POLICEMAN. Contagious?

JACK. Yes. It's canine strepto-klepto-coccus.

*(**JACK** pulls a surgical mask over his face.)*

POLICEMAN. Canine Strepto-klep... I've never heard of it.

JACK. Oh, it's a nasty disease. Makes you barking mad before it kills you. They're dropping like flies around here.

POLICEMAN. Oh my God.

> *(He steps away from the sleeping women.)*

JACK. Now, what brings you here, Officer?

POLICEMAN. *(Crossing to* **BARNEY***.)* I'm responding to an alarm call.

JACK. Oh yes, our friend Mr. Smith. The nurse here was feeding him

> *(Picking the bowl up off the floor and holding it up.)*

when she began to complain of feeling light-headed. She stood up and dropped the bowl of soup on him just before she passed out.

POLICEMAN. *(Kneeling down to examine the bracelet.)* Soup, eh? Yeah, that'd do it, alright. Any kind of liquid would be enough to screw up the electronics in this thing. I'll just have to reset it. Won't take a second.

> *(He fiddles with the bracelet for a moment and the beeping stops.)*

JACK. That's a relief.

POLICEMAN. You shouldn't have any more trouble with it – as long as you don't spill anything else on the poor guy.

> *(He stands up, looks at the two "bodies.")*

You're not just gonna leave those two like that, are you?

JACK. Why not? They look so comfortable together.

> *(The* **POLICEMAN** *gives him a look.)*

Anyway, you'd better get out of here. As I said, canine strepto-klepto-coccus is highly communicable.

POLICEMAN. Good point.

> *(He turns to leave when suddenly* **HARPER***, beginning to come to, lets out a protracted moan.)*

(Turning back.) What was that?

JACK. What was what?

POLICEMAN. That sound.

> **(BARNEY,** *in an effort to cover, lets out a hound-dog-like howl as before.)*

JACK. Oh, no! That's the first symptom! He's got it too!

> **(BARNEY** *howls again.)*

(To **POLICEMAN.***)* Quick! Save yourself!

POLICEMAN. I'm outta here!

> *(He bolts out upstage right. After he's gone,* **BARNEY** *and* **JACK** *share a sigh of relief.* **JACK** *pulls off the surgical mask and stethoscope and pockets them.)*

JACK. *(Brightly.)* That went well.

> **(BARNEY** *gives him a look.* **HARPER** *moans again. She begins to stir.)*

Quick – let's get Blanche away from her.

BARNEY. Good idea.

> *(Under the following, they each take one of* **BLANCHE***'s arms and half-carry her back to her chair upstage left.)*

Nice job getting rid of that cop, by the way. You'd make a great con artist.

JACK. I'm just a good businessman, that's all.

BARNEY. Potato, potahto.

> **(HARPER** *begins to wake up.* **BARNEY** *quickly scrambles back to his wheelchair and assumes the position.* **HARPER** *sits up slowly.)*

HARPER. What happened? What am I doing on the floor?

JACK. You fainted.

HARPER. I did? That's what I get for missing lunch.

> *(She begins to get up, but she's rather unsteady on her feet.* **JACK** *offers her an arm.)*

JACK. May I help?

> *(He guides her to the sofa and sits her down.)*

HARPER. Thank you, Mr. Newman. Now, where was I?

> *(Looking around blearily.)*

There was that annoying beeping…oh, yes – the security alarm!

JACK. It's all been taken care of. We had a little accident with Effward's soup and it set off the alarm. The police came and reset it.

HARPER. I see.

> *(Noticing the white coat he's wearing.)*

Why are you in that doctor's coat?

JACK. Huh?

> *(Looking down.)*

Oh, that.

> *(Closing the lab coat.)*

He's a very messy eater.

> *(He takes off the doctor's coat and tosses it on a chair.)*

HARPER. *(Peering over at the tray.)* It doesn't look like he's eaten much of anything. Let's see if we can't get some of this pudding down you, Mr. Smith.

> *(She picks up the pudding and a spoon.)*

JACK. *(Quickly.)* I don't think he's hungry, Nurse Harper.

HARPER. Ah, but this is pudding! Everybody likes pudding! Don't they, Mr. Smith?

> **(BARNEY** *turns away.)*

Oh, don't be like that. It's banana! Here comes the choo-choo!

> *(She moves the spoon toward his mouth, making chug-a-chug-a noises as she does so.* **BARNEY** *keeps his mouth shut.)*

Well, alright, if that's how you feel. Waste not want not.

(She eats a mouthful. JACK *gasps.)*

BARNEY. AAAGGHH!!

JACK. I think he wants it.

HARPER. *(Smacking her lips.)* Hmmm. It's a little lumpy today.

(To **BARNEY**.*)*

Changed your mind, have you? Very well, here you go!
(She picks up another spoon and plops some pudding into **BARNEY**'s *mouth.* **BARNEY** *grimaces, then swallows with difficulty.* JACK *buries his head in his hands.)*

There, that didn't hurt, now did it?

*(*BARNEY *glares at her balefully.)*

Would you like some more?

*(*BARNEY *slowly opens his mouth wide.* JACK *begins to sob quietly to himself.* HARPER *feeds* BARNEY *another mouthful.)*

Very good, Mr. Smith! It seems you have quite an appetite after all!

(She quickly spoons the rest of the pudding down his throat. As she's about to feed him the last spoonful, she stops and looks at it.)

My goodness this is lumpy.

(She inspects the pudding very closely. Slowly, she becomes aware of the fact that JACK *is hovering over her shoulder, inspecting the pudding as well. Beat.)*

JACK. Yes. Very lumpy. You should speak to Chef about that.

(Before she has a chance to turn back, **BARNEY** *quickly leans forward and downs the last of the pudding.)*

HARPER. *(Turning back to* **BARNEY** *and noticing the spoon is empty.)* The lumps don't seem to be bothering Mr. Smith. He's eaten it all up. Good boy!

> *(She pats him on the head, puts the bowl on the tray, and starts off.)*

I'll be back to change you out of those wet pants when I get a moment.

> *(She exits upstage left.)*

BARNEY. Congratulations, genius! Thanks to you, I'm a walking safety deposit box!

JACK. Don't worry. We'll get them back.

BARNEY. What are you suggesting, surgery?

JACK. No, just a little patience. Let nature take its course.

BARNEY. Well if that's your plan, you're going to need more than a little patience. All this pudding has got me so bunged up I haven't been to the can in days!

JACK. That's easily solved. We just need to get our hands on some laxatives.

BARNEY. Gee, you're just chock-full of fun ideas, aren't you? Where are we going to find laxatives?

JACK. Are you kidding? This is a retirement home! We've got enough laxatives in this place to blow a hole in the Hoover Dam!

BARNEY. That makes me feel so much better. And what do we do about Harper?

JACK. What do you mean?

BARNEY. That mouthful of pudding she took. For all we know, she could be walking around with a million bucks inside of her.

JACK. Well we don't know that for sure, those lumps could have just been…cornstarch.

BARNEY. I'm telling you right now, if any of our "lumps" are missing, they're coming out of your share.

JACK. Fine. Whatever. Now, sit tight while I scrounge up some ex-lax.

(**BARNEY** *groans.*)

Relax – it'll come out alright in the end.

BARNEY. You had to say it, didn't you?

(**BLANCHE** *wakes up.*)

BLANCHE. I must have nodded off. What did I miss?

BARNEY. Don't ask.

(**BLANCHE** *crosses downstage as* **JACK** *knocks on* **FLORA**'s *and* **ROSE**'s *door.*)

JACK. Ladies, can you join us out here a minute?

(**ROSE** *peeks out from her room.*)

ROSE. Is the coast clear?

JACK. Yes, come on, quickly!

(*She and* **FLORA** *enter and cross to the table downstage right.*)

FLORA. What can we do for you, Jack?

JACK. We have a bit of a situation on our hands, and we need your help.

ROSE. Of course.

FLORA. (*Looking at the now-empty table.*) What happened to all those lovely diamonds?

JACK. That's the situation.

BLANCHE. Oh no, you haven't lost them, have you?

JACK. No, no, we know exactly where they are.

(*With a look to* **BARNEY**.)

The problem is getting them back. That's where you come in.

ROSE. Anything we can do to help, Jack. What do you need?

JACK. Laxatives.

BLANCHE. (*To* **BARNEY**.) Dear God, you didn't *eat* them, did you?

BARNEY. It wasn't my idea!

FLORA. Why in the world would you do that?

JACK. It doesn't matter. The point is he did, and now we need to get them back. So, can you help?

ROSE, BLANCHE, & FLORA. Absolutely.

> *(As one, the three women reach into their purses and pull out an impressive store of ex-lax bars.)*

JACK. *(Deadpan.)* That ought to do it.

> *(The women busy themselves unwrapping the bars, breaking off squares and handing them to* **BARNEY**.*)*

ROSE. Here you go, Mr. Smith.

BARNEY. *(Taking a bite, almost gagging.)* Bleh! This stuff's disgusting!

ROSE. It beats Metamucil.

JACK. *(To* BARNEY.*)* Quit complaining and get it down you.

> *(HARPER enters. BARNEY slumps. ROSE deftly hides the ex-lax wrappers.)*

HARPER. What's going on here?

JACK. Mr. Smith was still hungry so we decided to give him some chocolate. He loves chocolate.

> *(JACK grabs some ex-lax and shoves it in BARNEY's mouth. BARNEY groans a little as he desperately tries to swallow.)*

See what I mean?

HARPER. Looks to me like he's in some distress.

> *(Taking the remaining squares of ex-lax from the table.)*

That's enough, Mr. Smith. Chocolate can be very hard on your digestion. Come to think of it, I don't believe I've taken you to the men's room since you got here. I'd better check your chart.

> *(HARPER exits upstage left.)*

JACK. Oh no. She stole our stash. Now what do we do?

ROSE. *(Opening her purse and producing another bar.)* Don't worry, dear, there's plenty more where that came from.

Here you go, this one's much tastier. It's creme de menthe.

(She hands it to **BARNEY** *who begrudgingly puts it in his mouth.)*

BARNEY. *(Grimacing as he chews.)* Yummy. How much of this do I need?

FLORA. Oh, two or three pieces usually does the trick for me.

JACK. Better eat the whole bar just to be safe.

BARNEY. *(In distress.)* I need something to chase this with.

JACK. *(Pulling his scotch from the window seat.)* This ought to do the trick.

(He hands **BARNEY** *the bottle.* **BARNEY** *takes a large swig.)*

Scotch and ex-lax. I think we've invented a new cocktail here.

BLANCHE. What'll we call it?

FLORA. The Highland Fling?

JACK. The Single Malt Quickstep?

ROSE. I know!

(Scottish accent.)

The Shitland Pony!

BLANCHE. Rose, please.

(Feeding **BARNEY.***)*

Come on, Mr. Effward, one more square, you can do it.

BARNEY. *(Eating another square.)* This stuff better work.

*(***HARPER** *enters with a covered tray.* **JACK** *hides the scotch bottle.* **BARNEY** *slumps.)*

HARPER. I was right about you, Mr. Smith. You haven't had a bowel movement in three days. Time to rectify that.

(She pulls off the cover on the tray and holds up a huge hypodermic needle and taps it in preparation. They all gasp, **BARNEY** *included.* **BARNEY,***

> *panic-stricken, starts to get up out of his chair.*
> **JACK** *shoves him back.)*

ROSE. What is that?

HARPER. Just what the doctor ordered - an extra strength, fast-acting laxative.

> *(She turns to* **BARNEY,** *pushes him on his side slightly, and pulls his pajama bottoms down a touch.)*

Now you're going to feel a little pinch, Mr. Smith.

JACK. *(Sotto.)* That's what they always say.

> *(She plunges the needle into his butt cheek with gusto. The others all look away.* **BARNEY** *howls in pain.)*

HARPER. There we are. All done. Now, sit tight. I'll be back to check on you shortly.

> *(She exits upstage left.* **BARNEY** *sobs.)*

BARNEY. *(Through his sobs.)* I should have gone to jail while I had the chance!

JACK. Stop your whining. We've got to get prepared.

BARNEY. For what?

JACK. The retrieval, what do you think?

ROSE. Right. We've got to be ready. How are we going to…?

BLANCHE. I know just what we need.

> *(She begins to exit upstage left.)*

JACK. You better hurry, Blanche, we don't know how long we've got.

> *(***BLANCHE** *rushes off.)*

BARNEY. Give me that bottle.

> *(***JACK** *hands him the scotch and* **BARNEY** *takes a swig.)*

JACK. You sure you should mix your medications like that?

BARNEY. I'll take my chances.

JACK. Remember what's at stake here. That's ten million bucks in diamonds you're sitting on.

ROSE. Literally.

JACK. It's worth a little discomfort to get them back, don't you think?

BARNEY. A little discomfort? Did you see the size of that needle?

(BLANCHE enters carrying a large, red spaghetti strainer.)

BLANCHE. This should do the trick!

ROSE. A spaghetti strainer! That's perfect.

(BLANCHE gives the strainer to BARNEY.)

BLANCHE. *(Holding up a pair of garishly-colored rubber gloves.)* I thought these might come in handy too.

BARNEY. Good thinking. Hand them over.

JACK. Not so fast.

(He takes the gloves from BLANCHE and puts them on.)

BARNEY. What are you doing?

JACK. You don't think I'm going to let you do this alone, do you?

BARNEY. You've got to be kidding! Can't a guy have a little privacy?

JACK. Not with ten million bucks at stake.

BARNEY. Forget it. Not going to happen.

(JACK grabs the strainer from BARNEY's hand.)

JACK. Fine. Suit yourself.

BARNEY. *(Rising.)* I can't have you in there with me, I have a hard enough time using public urinals.

JACK. Too bad.

BARNEY. Give that back!

(He begins to chase JACK around the room, and suddenly freezes as a cramp seizes him.)

BARNEY. *(Cont.)* Ooh! She wasn't kidding when she said "fast acting"!

> *(He races to the bathroom door.* **JACK** *is on his heels.)*

JACK. Mind the fort, ladies!

> *(They exit into the bathroom. A beat.)*

ROSE. I guess this is where the shit hits the fan.

BLANCHE. Rose!

> *(***HARPER'S*** *voice is heard offstage.)*

HARPER. *(Offstage.)* I'm coming as fast as I can, Mrs. Draper.

BLANCHE. Oh my!

> *(To* **FLORA.***)*

Keep her occupied.

FLORA. Yes. Right. Who?

BLANCHE. Oh my goodness – Nurse Harper!

FLORA. Right.

> *(She rushes upstage left as* **HARPER** *enters.* **FLORA** *flings her arms around her and jumps her up and down a little.)*
>
> *(Throughout the following,* **BLANCHE** *helps* **ROSE** *to get into the wheelchair. She covers her with the blanket and* **BARNEY***'s hat and sunglasses.* **ROSE** *slumps in the chair à la* **BARNEY***.)*

HARPER. Mrs. Parker! What an earth are you doing?

> *(She extricates herself.)*

FLORA. I just felt it was time for a random act of kindness. You are so good to us, we'd be lost without you. Tell me, is there anything I can do to make your day a little easier?

HARPER. *(Nonplussed.)* Well…that depends.

FLORA. Ooh, Depends! I know exactly where they are.

> *(She turns toward the closet.)*

HARPER. No, Mrs. Parker, that's not what I meant.

(Turning to the wheelchair.)

So. How is our patient doing?

(Coming closer.)

Mr. Smith?

FLORA. *(Following her.)* He's fine.

BLANCHE. Just having a nap.

HARPER. That's odd. He should be about ready to visit the little boys room by now.

BLANCHE. We'll let you know as soon as anything happens, Nurse Harper.

(There follows an extended series of flatulent noises emanating from the bathroom. None of the women react. An uncomfortable pause.)

HARPER. Who is in there?

BLANCHE. That would be...

*(She looks at **ROSE** and then back to **HARPER**.)*

Rose.

HARPER. My goodness.

FLORA. *(Confidentially.)* I think it was the chili.

HARPER. I see. Alright. I'll be back shortly.

(She exits upstage left.)

ROSE. *(Lifting up her head, mortified.)* Did you have to say it was me?

*(The bathroom door opens and **BARNEY** comes out, dejectedly. A second later **JACK** appears in the doorway, eyes watering, overcome by fumes. He waves his hand in front of his face weakly as he crosses to the sofa, desperate for a little fresh air.)*

BLANCHE. Well?

JACK. False alarm.

ROSE. But it sounded so promising.

*(**BARNEY** gives her a tap.)*

BARNEY. Hey. Get out of my chair.

> (**ROSE** *hauls herself up and* **BARNEY** *sits in the wheelchair.* **BLANCHE**, *meanwhile, sits on the sofa and promptly nods off.*)

ROSE. *(Giving him back his disguise.)* Here you go, Mr. Smith.

FLORA. How long do you think this is going to take?

BARNEY. *(Overcoming a bit of cramp.)* Not very.

FLORA. Well, while we're waiting I think I'll get started on a new necklace.

> *(She sits and opens her bag of materials.)*

ROSE. Good idea. If my sales projections are accurate, we're going to need some more product tout de suite.

JACK. Why are you bothering with all that? Once we get the stones back, we'll all be set for life.

ROSE. It's not about the money.

FLORA. No, Jack, it's just so exciting. Since Rose set up the – what is it called?

ROSE. Website –

FLORA. Website this morning, we've had over three thousand visitors!

ROSE. That's right, Jack, we've gone viral!

JACK. So you're going to stay here, running your little business?

FLORA. Of course. This is our home. Where else would we go?

JACK. I think I'll start by taking Blanche on a nice trip somewhere. What do you think about that, honey?

> (**BLANCHE** *is down for the count.*)

Well, we can talk about it later.

BARNEY. Waste of money if you ask me. What's the point of taking her on a trip if she's going to sleep through – oh, speaking of trips…!

> *(He dashes off toward the bathroom.)*

ROSE. Bon voyage!

(*JACK begins to run after him, holding the strainer in front of himself.*)

HARPER. *(Offstage.)* No, Mrs. Draper, you couldn't have seen him. Elvis died in 1977.

JACK. *(Racing back to* **ROSE.**) Oh no. The SS is back.

(*Giving her the strainer.*)

Hold this!

(*To the sleeping* **BLANCHE.**) Sorry about this, honey.

(*He hauls her up and deposits her in the wheelchair, quickly disguising her with* **BARNEY**'s *hat and glasses.*)

BARNEY. *(Opening the bathroom door.)* STRAINER!!!!!!!!!!!!

JACK. *(Echoing.)* Strainer!!

(*He grabs the strainer from* **ROSE** *and bolts into the bathroom, closing the door.* **HARPER** *enters.*)

HARPER. How's our patient doing now?

ROSE. *(Brightly.)* Sleeping soundly.

HARPER. How odd.

(*She crosses to the wheelchair and taps* **BLANCHE** *on the shoulder.*)

Are you alright Mr. Smith?

BLANCHE. *(Waking up with a start.)* Sorry?

(*Taking off the glasses.*)

Oh. How did I get here?

HARPER. I was just about to ask you the very same thing. Where's Mr. Smith?

BLANCHE. I have no idea.

FLORA. Who's Mr. Smith?

ROSE. You know, Flora, the man in the wheelchair.

FLORA. Oh yes of course, he's in the bathroom, getting our money back.

HARPER. I beg your pardon?

ROSE. She's a little confused.

HARPER. How did he get in there?

ROSE. Jack took him in there.

FLORA. He had to go in a hurry.

HARPER. For heaven's sake.

> *(She marches to the bathroom door and knocks sharply.)*

Is everything alright in there?

> *(The toilet flushes and the door opens.* **JACK** *stands there with the strainer in his hand.)*

JACK. Fine and dandy, thanks.

HARPER. Where's Mr. Smith?

JACK. He's fine. He's, umm…otherwise engaged. He's going to be a while.

HARPER. What are you doing with that strainer?

JACK. I thought it might come in handy.

> *(Beat.)*

I didn't want him to strain himself.

HARPER. *(Snatching the strainer.)* Give me that. I'll be back in a minute. Do try and behave yourselves while I'm gone.

JACK. *(Clicking his heels.)* Jawold!

HARPER. *(Under her breath as she exits upstage left)* …I'm starting to re-think my views on euthanasia…

BLANCHE. She's taking that strainer back to the kitchen.

ROSE. Remind me never to eat spaghetti in this place again.

JACK. Don't worry, that thing has been thoroughly sterilized. They've got stuff in that bathroom that could clean up a toxic waste dump.

ROSE. Speaking of which – did everything come out alright?

> *(***JACK*** *fishes the diamonds out from his pocket and holds them out.)*

JACK. See for yourself.

(ROSE and BLANCHE gather around, oohing and aahing. FLORA puts away her jewelry materials.)

BLANCHE. Look how sparkly they are.

FLORA. *(Crossing with her bag of jewelry.)* They're so beautiful!

JACK. Best I've ever seen.

ROSE. Pity we have to sell them, really. They are exquisite.

(The bathroom door opens and BARNEY enters, leaning on the door jam, recovering.)

JACK. How are you feeling?

BARNEY. Just call me Vesuvius. You got the stones?

JACK. Right here.

(JACK holds them out to show him.)

BARNEY. Good. Try not to feed them to anybody else, will you? Did you get them all?

JACK. All but one. There are only nineteen here.

BARNEY. You know what that means, don't you?

ROSE. Nineteen? Where's the twentieth?

JACK. We lost it.

ROSE. Where?

BARNEY. Inside Nurse Harper.

BLANCHE. *What?*

JACK. I'll explain later.

BARNEY. Yeah, we've got more important things to deal with. Let's get the rest of those stones sorted out.

VOICE. *(Offstage.)* Nurse Harper to the annex immediately. Nurse Harper to the annex, please.

JACK. The annex? Good. She'll be out of our hair for a while.

(JACK crosses to the table and dumps the diamonds down. Everyone else follows excitedly.)

BARNEY. Where are the appraisals?

(JACK reaches into his pants.)

JACK. Right here.

(He pulls out the appraisals and flattens them out in a pile on the table.)

ROSE. What were they doing down there?

JACK. It's a long story.

BLANCHE. Not that long, dear.

JACK. Oh thank you very much.

BARNEY. Enough!

(To **JACK**.*)*

Alright, you read off the serial numbers and I'll find the right appraisal.

JACK. Right.

(He sits at the table and pulls out the loupe and gemstone holder, inspecting the first stone. **FLORA**, **BLANCHE**, *and* **ROSE** *sit at the table with him.* **BARNEY** *deserts his wheelchair and crosses to* **JACK**.*)*

BARNEY. Move over, Flora, I gotta get in here.

(He picks up the pile of appraisals.)

JACK. *(Examining.)* My my, what a gorgeous stone.

BARNEY. What's the serial number?

*(***HARPER** *enters upstage left.)*

HARPER. Was that page for me?

(They all leap to their feet with a cry of surprise and turn to her in shock.)

Mr. Smith! What are you doing out of your wheelchair?

(Beat. **JACK** *turns to* **BARNEY**, *as if seeing him for the first time.)*

JACK. It's a miracle! He's been healed. Hallelujah!

(They throw their arms in the air like it's a Baptist revival meeting. There is a lot of activity.)

ALL. *(Breaking into a round of the Hallelujah chorus.)* Hallelujah! Hallelujah! Hallelujah!

HARPER. Okay, okay cut it out! That's enough!

> *(To* **BARNEY**.*)*

I should have known this was all an act. Once a con man, always a con man –

JACK. Nurse Harper –

HARPER. *(Turning to* **JACK**.*)* And you're just as bad. I told them not to put you two together. You're cut from the same cloth – a dirty one. Now, before I call the police, I want to know what you're up to.

JACK. Up to?

HARPER. Don't play me for a fool, Mr. Newman, I'm on to you.

JACK. I don't know what you're talking about.

HARPER. Okay. Blanche, why don't *you* tell me what's going on?

BLANCHE. We were playing a game of –

> *(She falls asleep.)*

JACK. Euchre!

FLORA. Euchre? What about the diamonds?

> *(They all freeze in horror.)*

HARPER. Diamonds?

JACK. *(Quickly.)* No, I told you before, Flora, *hearts* were trump, not diamonds. We're never going to win a hand if you can't keep that straight. Shall we play?

> *(They all sit down.* **HARPER** *looks down at the table, which is bare except for the appraisals.)*

HARPER. If you're playing euchre where are your cards?

> *(They all start looking for the cards.* **FLORA** *starts patting* **JACK***'s thighs.)*

JACK. Flora! What are you doing?

FLORA. Looking for the cards.

HARPER. In his pants?

FLORA. Well, that's where he had these.

(She picks up the appraisals.)

JACK. Flora!!

HARPER. What are those?

*(She takes them from **FLORA** and reads the first one. The others freeze in horror.)*

Aha! Diamonds, eh?

(Riffling through the pages.)

A few million dollars worth, by the looks of these. Anyone want to tell me what this is about?

(Silence.)

Fine. If you're not going to talk to me, we'll let the police sort it out.

(She starts to go upstage right.)

BARNEY. Just a minute, Nurse Harper.

HARPER. *(Turning back.)* He speaks!

BARNEY. I wouldn't be calling the police if I were you.

HARPER. Why is that?

BARNEY. Because you could end up in as much trouble as the rest of us.

HARPER. Oh really? What kind of trouble would that be?

BARNEY. You could be charged with theft.

HARPER. Is that so? And what am I supposed to have stolen?

BARNEY. My pudding.

HARPER. I beg your pardon?

JACK. That mouthful of banana pudding you helped yourself to just happened to contain a five-hundred thousand dollar diamond!

HARPER. *(Stunned.)* What? You mean…?

(She puts a hand on her belly.)

JACK. Yes. At this moment you have the most expensive digestive tract on the planet.

HARPER. Ohmigod.

BARNEY. You call the police and you're going to have a hard time explaining what that thing is doing rolling around in your innards.

HARPER. But I'm innocent! I didn't know anything about any diamonds.

BARNEY. That's your story. We could just as easily tell the cops that that half-million dollar diamond is your share of the loot.

JACK. You know what they say, Nurse Harper, possession's nine-tenths of the law –

BARNEY. And at the moment you're in possession of some very incriminating evidence.

HARPER. But I –

(Looking around, frantically.)

I've got to get it out of me!

JACK. Oh I wouldn't worry, Nurse Harper, the police will take care of that.

*(Turning to **BARNEY**.)*

What do you think they'll do, Barney?

BARNEY. An endoscopy, for starters.

JACK. And if that doesn't work, you know what the next step is…?

BARNEY. Yeah.

JACK & BARNEY. Cavity search.

HARPER. *(Collapsing into a chair.)* Aaah.

BARNEY. Don't get your stethoscope in a twist, there's an easy way out of this. In fact it could be very lucrative, if you're willing to play along.

HARPER. Play along?

BARNEY. Yup. You just pretend you never saw any of this. As far as you're concerned, I'm still the turnip in the wheelchair. You forget the last five minutes ever happened and we'll agree to do the same; that way we get to keep what's ours and you –

(Pointing at her gut.)

get to keep what's yours.

>   *(Beat.)*

JACK. Imagine what you could do with half a million dollars, Nurse Harper.

ROSE. You know how unhappy you are here. Just think, you could leave this place.

BLANCHE. Have a life somewhere.

FLORA. Somewhere with no responsibilities...

ROSE. No Mrs. Draper...

FLORA. No Depends.

HARPER. *(Dreamily.)* No Depends...

JACK. So what about it?

HARPER. *(Coming back to reality.)* Sounds good to me.

BARNEY. Then it's a deal?

HARPER. Not quite. There's still one problem.

BARNEY. What's that?

HARPER. I've got no proof that I actually swallowed this diamond, let alone that it's worth what you say it is. We'll just have to wait until the stone...reappears...and if it does, then we have a deal. Agreed?

>   *(Everyone looks at **BARNEY**.)*

BARNEY. Agreed.

>   *(She turns to go.)*

In the meantime, Nurse Harper, not a word to anyone about this.

HARPER. *(Feigning innocence.)* About what, Mr. Smith?

>   *(She smiles and begins to exit.)*

ROSE. *(Pulling the ex-lax from her purse.)* Nurse Harper!

>   *(**HARPER** turns back. **ROSE** holds out the offering.)*

I thought you might appreciate a little help with your... exit strategy.

>   *(**HARPER** takes the ex-lax.)*

HARPER. Ooh, creme de menthe. Thanks.

> *(She exits.)*

JACK. Right. Where were we?

ROSE. *(Holding up the papers.)* I've got the appraisals.

JACK. Great. Who's got the stones?

FLORA. Stones? What stones?

JACK. The diamonds, Flora.

FLORA. Oh yes, the diamonds. Now where did they get to?

> *(A beat. They look at one another.)*

ROSE. Blanche must have them.

> *(She shakes **BLANCHE** gently.)*

Blanche, dear. Wakey, wakey.

BLANCHE. *(Rousing herself.)* Hmm?

ROSE. Where are the diamonds?

BLANCHE. What?

BARNEY. The diamonds. What did you do with them?

BLANCHE. I don't have them.

JACK. Are you sure?

BLANCHE. *(Turning out her pockets.)* Last I saw of them they were on the table.

ROSE. They didn't end up on the floor, did they?

> *(**JACK** looks under the table.)*

JACK. Nothing here.

BARNEY. Good God. They didn't disappear into thin air. Somebody's got to have them.

JACK. Well don't look at me. I was busy examining the stone.

BARNEY. Exactly! You had one in your hand!

JACK. Which I dropped on the table so I could put away my loupe. What were you doing?

BARNEY. I was reading the appraisals. So that leaves you!

> *(He points a finger at **FLORA**.)*

FLORA. Leaves me where?

BARNEY. You're the only one who could have taken them.

FLORA. Taken what?

BARNEY. The diamonds!!

FLORA. What diamonds?

BARNEY. Oh for God's sake!! Can't you remember anything?!

ROSE. Stop yelling at her, she didn't take anything.

BARNEY. What's in there?

> (**BARNEY** *points at* **FLORA**'s *jewelry bag, which is in her hand.*)

FLORA. My jewelry things.

BARNEY. Open it.

ROSE. Now just a minute! Who are you to…

JACK. Hang on, Rose. He's got a point. Maybe she…got confused and put them in there without realizing it.

BLANCHE. Yes, she may have forgotten.

FLORA. Forgotten what?

ROSE. Do you mind, Flora dear, if we take a quick look at your jewelry bag?

FLORA. No, not at all.

> (**ROSE** *snatches it from her, quickly pulls it open, and spills out the contents on the table.* **BARNEY** *and* **JACK** *paw through it.*)

JACK. Nothing here but paste.

> (*He stuffs everything back in the bag.*)

BARNEY. This is ridiculous! Somebody picked the damn things up. Alright, I'm going to have to frisk all of you.

BLANCHE. What?

FLORA. *(Overlapping.)* Frisk us?

JACK. *(Overlapping.)* Now just a minute!

ROSE. *(Overlapping.)* Not on your life!

BARNEY. Let's start with you.

(He steps toward **ROSE**, *who brandishes her cane at him.)*

ROSE. Hold it right there, Buster! You lay one finger on me and you'll find out what elder abuse *really* means! Who are you to be casting aspersions on the rest of us? There's only one criminal in this room, and that's you! Come on Flora, we're not putting up with this.

FLORA. *(Taking her bag from* **JACK**.*)* Hmmph!

(She and **ROSE** *hobble off in high dudgeon to their room.* **BARNEY** *turns to* **BLANCHE**, *who has fallen asleep. He steps toward her, but* **JACK** *intercepts.)*

JACK. Don't even think about it. If anyone's going to frisk her it's me!

*(***JACK** *gives the sleeping* **BLANCHE** *a gentle pat down.)*

BARNEY. So?

JACK. She's clean.

BARNEY. Well, where the hell are they? They've got to be somewhere!

JACK. You sure you didn't eat them again?

BARNEY. Oh, shut up!

JACK. Are they in your pants?

BARNEY. No. Are they in yours? Everything else seems to be.

JACK. Very funny. Come here.

BARNEY. What for?

JACK. Like Rose said, there's only one criminal in this place. If anybody scooped up those stones my money's on you. Now turn out your pockets.

BARNEY. What?

JACK. Well, you're the one who wants to frisk everybody. Nobody's frisked you yet.

BARNEY. Nobody's frisked you either.

(A brief standoff.)

BARNEY. *(Cont.)* Come on, let's get this over with.

> *(Standing nose to nose they begin to frisk one another. They begin by patting each other's backs, working their way down to their back pockets.)*

JACK. *(Highly uncomfortable.)* Do you mind?

BARNEY. Sorry.

> *(They work down each other's torsos to their front pockets.)*

JACK. What have you got in here?

BARNEY. *(Indignant.)* What do you think?

> *(JACK's hand retreats as if by electric shock.)*

JACK. Aaaghh!

> *(BARNEY gets down on his knees.)*

What are you doing now?!

BARNEY. We've got to be thorough.

> *(He begins to pat down one of his legs.)*

JACK. Oh, for God's sake!

> *(Just as BARNEY reaches one of JACK's ankles, MORTIMER enters upstage right. He is wearing a surgical mask, gloves, and a hospital gown over his suit. He carries his briefcase.)*

MORTIMER. Excuse me!

> *(JACK and BARNEY shriek. JACK turns toward MORTIMER and BARNEY drops to the floor like a stone.)*

JACK. Who the hell are you?

MORTIMER. It's me, Dr. Anderson. Mortimer. I'm here to see my client. What's happened to him?

JACK. Oh. Yes. He's...er –

> *(BARNEY begins barking.)*

He's had another episode, I'm afraid. That pesky canine strepto-klepto-coccus just won't go away.

(BARNEY gets on all fours, wags his tail, lifts his leg as if to pee on MORTIMER's foot, and does his best dog impression.)

Excuse me a moment.

(Turning to BARNEY.)

Bad dog!

(He hauls BARNEY up and plops him back in his wheelchair.)

There we go. Back to your kennel.

(Turning to MORTIMER.)

Now, can I be of some assistance?

MORTIMER. Yes, as a matter of fact. I need to discuss the details of Mr. Smith's transfer.

JACK. Transfer?

MORTIMER. Yes, haven't you heard? All the charges against him have been stayed. He's a free man.

(BARNEY lets out a howl of giddy delight, which he quickly disguises as a dog howl.)

JACK. You're kidding. How did that happen?

MORTIMER. *(With satisfaction.)* I got them on a technicality. They screwed up the search warrant. All the evidence connected with it had to be thrown out, which has left the prosecution with no case. The judge had no choice but to cut him loose.

(Some dog-like panting is heard emanating from BARNEY's direction, along with a few happy yips.)

Is he alright?

JACK. Yes, he's fine.

(Turning to BARNEY.)

Down boy.

MORTIMER. So the first thing I need to do is get rid of this bracelet.

*(He punches a code into his mobile phone and then bends down and pulls the bracelet off **BARNEY**'s ankle.)*

JACK. You can shut that thing off with a mobile phone?

MORTIMER. If you know what you're doing. Now, as for transport: due to Mr. Smith's medical condition, I've arranged for an ambulance to pick him up first thing tomorrow morning.

JACK. What? No!

MORTIMER. Why not?

JACK. We've been through this, Mr. Mortimer. He's in no condition to be moved.

MORTIMER. Don't worry, they are completely aware of his condition and he will be put in an isolation unit.

JACK. Where's he going?

MORTIMER. Well our choices were rather limited. Although Mr. Smith may be a free man, he is also flat broke. We had no option but to put him in a government facility.

JACK. Government facility?

MORTIMER. Yes. It's called Departure Point.

*(**BARNEY** whimpers like a dog.)*

Gee, he's got it bad, doesn't he?

JACK. Worst case I've ever seen.

MORTIMER. Well, thank you very much, Dr. Anderson. Congratulations, Mr. Smith. I'll be in touch.

*(**MORTIMER** exits upstage right.)*

JACK. So what are you waiting for?

BARNEY. What do you mean?

JACK. You've got your get-out-of-jail-free card. If I were you I'd be getting the hell out of here.

BARNEY. *(Beginning to search the room.)* Not without my diamonds, I'm not.

JACK. Those are *our* diamonds you're talking about.

BARNEY. They're nobody's diamonds unless we find them
    before someone else does.

JACK. *(Joining in the search.)* Well we better get on with it or
    we're going to be sharing another room at Departure
    Point.

   (The lights fade.)

Scene II

(The next morning. All the crime scene tape is gone. Things are back to normal. **BARNEY** *sits at the table going through a pile of clothing, searching through all the pockets. He's been up all night and is quite distraught. A breakfast tray, untouched, sits on the table next to him.* **ROSE** *is on the sofa monitoring her website on the iPad.* **HARPER** *enters from upstage right. She crosses to the table and picks up the tray.)*

HARPER. No appetite this morning, Mr. Smith? We can't send you off on an empty stomach.

*(**BARNEY** emits a low growl.)*

Everybody's so grumpy this morning for some reason.

ROSE. So Nurse Harper – any er –

(Patting her tummy.)

– movement?

HARPER. Nothing yet.

(The iPad pings loudly.)

ROSE. Ooh, good! There's that "ping" again. We just sold another one, Flora.

FLORA. Goodness, I'll never be able to keep up with the demand. If this continues we'll have to hire some children in southeast Asia.

ROSE. *(Appalled.)* Flora!

FLORA. What?

HARPER. What are you two on about?

FLORA. Rose set up a website to sell my jewelry.

ROSE. We just started yesterday and they're selling like hotcakes.

HARPER. May I have a look?

ROSE. Of course.

(She shows her the iPad.)

HARPER. Oh, those earrings are lovely.

ROSE. Aren't they? But I'm afraid they're sold.

HARPER. Oh, that's okay, I'm not really in the market – although come to think of it, now that I'm coming into a little money, perhaps I could treat myself... Ooh, how much are those?

ROSE. Two hundred and fifty plus shipping. We have an account with UPS. Actually they're coming by later today to pick up our first shipment. That reminds me, I'd better tell them at reception.

(She bustles off upstage right.)

HARPER. *(To* **FLORA.***)* And you made all this yourself?

FLORA. I did.

HARPER. Really? I've underestimated you, Flora. You're very talented.

FLORA. Thank you.

HARPER. Ooh, look at this necklace, isn't it gorgeous?

FLORA. Yes, that's my favorite. They're not real diamonds, of course. But they are beautiful, aren't they?

*(***BARNEY***'s ears perk up.)*

HARPER. Seven hundred and fifty dollars. That's quite a hefty pricetag.

FLORA. Well, it was a lot of work setting all those stones. There are nineteen of them, you know.

*(***BARNEY*** *gasps.)*

(The iPad pings loudly.)

HARPER. Ooh! Sounds like you just made another sale.

BARNEY. *(Rushing over.)* Can I have a peek?

HARPER. Sure.

(She shows it to him.)

Isn't that lovely?

BARNEY. *(Feigning nonchalance.)* Not bad for costume jewelry.

HARPER. *(To* FLORA.*)* I can buy these right off the website, can I?

FLORA. Yes, or just call our toll free number. 1-800-BLING ME!

HARPER. Catchy.

ROSE. *(Entering.)* Come on, Flora. We better pack up these pieces we've sold before the UPS man arrives.

FLORA. Right you are.

> *(She picks up her stuff and follows* ROSE *into their room.)*

HARPER. What a couple of canny grannies they turned out to be.

> *(She hands the iPad to* BARNEY, *picks up* BARNEY*'s tray, and suddenly stops dead.)*

Ohmigod!

> *(She puts the tray back down.)*

(Excited.) This is it!

> *(She bolts into the bathroom. As soon as she's gone,* BARNEY *crosses to the phone and dials frantically.)*

BARNEY. 1-800-BLING ME... Yes, I'm calling about item number

> *(Checking the iPad.)*

6623 on your website... $750 plus shipping...the name on the credit card? Just a second...

> *(He races into his room and right back out with a wallet. He picks up the receiver again.)*

The name on the card is Jack Newman...the number is...5122-0990-2435-1100...expires 08/21.

> *(The bathroom opens and a deflated* HARPER *appears in the doorway, unseen by* BARNEY.*)*

I just want to make sure I have the correct item here, it's the necklace with the nineteen stones.... That's the one… Shipping address? Box 1200, Correio Centrale, Rio de Janeiro, Brazil… It'll be there when? In two days?

> *(To himself.)*

Good. So will I.

> *(He hangs up, dances a little jig, and barks with glee, then turns to see* **HARPER** *staring at him. He stops dead.)*

HARPER. So you're reneging on your deal?

BARNEY. Why not? If that idiot Flora is stupid enough to sell a nine and a half million dollar necklace for seven hundred and fifty bucks, who am I to say no?

HARPER. I see.

BARNEY. You got a problem with that?

HARPER. No… I'm not saying that.

BARNEY. Then what are you saying?

HARPER. I'm saying…

> *(Pleading.)*

Take me with you.

BARNEY. What?

HARPER. Take me with you, *please!* If I spend five more minutes in this place I'm going to lose what's left of my sanity.

BARNEY. Sorry. I'm used to travelling solo.

HARPER. You'll have an easier time getting out of the country with me on your arm.

> *(She takes her glasses off.)*

BARNEY. True.

HARPER. I mean, nine and a half million bucks is a lot of money. You're going to need help spending it.

BARNEY. Perhaps…

> *(**HARPER** un-clips her hair and shakes it free.)*

Oh…

HARPER. And then there's the little matter of the half-mill in my...carry-on baggage.

BARNEY. What about it?

HARPER. I'm going to need some help investing it. When it comes to the stock market, I'm a total virgin.

> *(She rips off her uniform and reveals some super-sexy lingerie underneath.)*

So what do you say?

BARNEY. *(Gawping.)* Habadehabadehabadeh.

HARPER. I'll take that as a yes.

> *(She holds out her hand.* **BARNEY** *takes it.)*

Come on, let me help you pack.

> *(**BARNEY** begins dancing and humming a samba tune.* **HARPER** *joins in. They dance off into* **JACK**'s *room and close the door. Beat.* **JACK** *and* **BLANCHE** *enter from upstage left.)*

JACK. I smell like dead fish.

BLANCHE. I told you jumping into that dumpster would be a waste of time.

JACK. We've looked everywhere else.

BLANCHE. *(Sinking on to the sofa, despondent.)* Oh dear. What are we going to do?

> *(There is another announcement over the intercom.)*

VOICE. *(Offstage.)* Flora Parker to reception. There's a UPS man here for a pick up. Flora Parker to reception please.

> *(The door opens and* **ROSE** *and* **FLORA** *enter.* **FLORA** *carries a few packages, packed up and ready for delivery.* **ROSE** *picks up her iPad from the table.)*

FLORA. *(To* **ROSE**.*)* We got these ready just in the nick of time, didn't we?

> *(Hustling upstage right.)*

I'm coming, Mr. UPS...

(She exits.)

ROSE. *(To* JACK.*)* You're back.

JACK. *(Pulling a piece of lettuce from his pocket.)* Yes. And somewhat the worse for wear.

ROSE. Pooh. What's that smell?

BLANCHE. Jack decided to go dumpster-diving.

JACK. Leave no stone un-turned.

ROSE. And did the stones turn up?

JACK. I wish.

(Looking around.)

Hey, what happened to Effward?

ROSE. He was just here a few minutes ago.

JACK. Did they ship him off to Departure Point already?

BLANCHE. We didn't even get to say goodbye.

JACK. Unless we find those diamonds, we'll be saying hello to him soon enough.

(FLORA re-enters as ROSE's iPad pings.)

ROSE. I've got a message here from a "Lois H." Who's that?

(She pushes a button.)

It's a text…

(Reading.)

On our way to Rio. Have a nice life, suckers.

JACK. What the hell…?

ROSE. Just a minute, there's more. It's a photo…ohmigod.

BLANCHE. What is it?

ROSE. It's a selfie of Nurse Harper and Barney in the back of a taxi. What are they doing?

(She shows them the iPad.)

JACK. Giving us the finger! Those sonsabitches.

(He suddenly races into his room. A beat.)

FLORA. I don't understand. What's happened?

JACK. *(Returning.)* He's gone.

BLANCHE. What?

JACK. He's done a runner.

FLORA. Who?

JACK. Effward. The room's been trashed and the window's wide open. He's taken off.

FLORA. With Nurse Ratched?

ROSE. Who would have thought?

BLANCHE. Are you sure?

JACK. Of course I'm sure. He's cleaned me out! He's taken my suitcase, my clothes, my wallet.

BLANCHE. But why would he leave now? Before we found the – oh no!

ROSE. He's stolen the diamonds, hasn't he? That thieving bastard!

(She sits at the table, putting her iPad down.)

He must have had them this whole time.

JACK. That doesn't make sense. If he had the stones he would have taken off the second Mortimer removed his ankle bracelet. No, something else must have happened.

(The iPad pings loudly.)

FLORA. Oh goody, we sold another one.

(She crosses to the table to have a look.)

JACK. Sold another what?

ROSE. Another piece of jewelry from our website.

FLORA. We've sold four just this morning.

ROSE. Five, Flora dear. Your diamond necklace sold just as we were packing up the boxes. It came through on my laptop, remember?

JACK. Diamond necklace?

FLORA. They're not real diamonds, of course. But it's a very pretty piece, if I say so myself. Here, have a look.

(She shows the screen to JACK, *who glances at it and does a double-take. He starts counting the stones with his finger on the screen.)*

Lovely stones, aren't they? They almost look real.

JACK. Seventeen, eighteen, nineteen…

(Breathless.)

Flora, you didn't show this to Effward by any chance, did you?

FLORA. No.

JACK. Thank goodness.

FLORA. Nurse Harper did.

JACK. What?

BLANCHE. Oh no!

JACK. And where is this necklace now?

FLORA. Oh, that nice UPS man just took it away.

JACK. We've got to stop him!

ROSE. Too late. He just left.

JACK. Oh, no…

BLANCHE. You mean Barney bought our diamonds?

JACK. Yes, for seven hundred and fifty bucks.

FLORA. Plus shipping.

ROSE. Talk about a steal.

FLORA. Have I got a deal for you!

JACK. Shut up, Flora!

ROSE. I knew he'd find a way to screw us over.

BLANCHE. We have to stop him. He's stolen your identity. We've got to call the police!

JACK. And tell them what? The minute we point the finger at Effward he'll tell them we were in on it.

ROSE. That's right. We can't call the police. We'll end up in the slammer right beside him.

JACK. You said it, Rose. He's screwed us good and proper. It's over.

BLANCHE. It can't be. There must be something we can do!

JACK. There is one thing…

BLANCHE. *(Hopefully.)* What's that?

JACK. *(Deflated.)* Pack our bags. Looks like we're moving out after all.

> *(The lights fade as the four of them begin to exit dejectedly into their rooms.)*

Scene III

(Transition light and sound. It is a few days later. In a melancholy light **ROSE** *and* **FLORA** *enter, wearing coats and hats and wheeling their luggage. They stop outside their door.* **BLANCHE** *enters next, also in her coat and with luggage. She stops as well. Finally* **JACK** *enters and holds up his only possession – a toothbrush. Lights come up as they all cross to sit in the room.)*

ROSE. *(Checking her watch.)* The shuttle bus is late.

BLANCHE. *(Weeping.)* It's like we're being thrown out of our own home.

FLORA. But we are, dear.

JACK. Let's look at the bright side.

ROSE. What bright side?

JACK. Well, now that I'm broke, at least I've gotten my family off my back. They've cancelled the competency proceedings and basically disowned me.

FLORA. Disowned you? That's terrible.

JACK. Good riddance to them, I say. I've got all the family I need right here.

ROSE. You're quite right, Jack, at least we'll all still be together.

BLANCHE. Yes, but it won't be the same.

ROSE. No, true; this place may not be perfect, but it's a paradise compared to Departure Point.

BLANCHE. *(Bawling.)* Oh, I don't want to go!

*(***JACK** *puts an arm around her and comforts her.)*

JACK. Don't cry, sweetheart.

BLANCHE. It just makes my blood boil to think we're getting shipped off to that smelly, rotten place while those two are sitting on some beach in Rio drinking Mai Tais.

ROSE. Can you get Mai Tais in Brazil?

JACK. With ten million bucks you can get anything you want.

FLORA. *(Fanning herself.)* I wish that bus would just get here. I'm overheating. Oof.

ROSE. Take off your scarf, dear.

FLORA. *(Taking it off.)* Yes, I don't suppose I need this. It's quite mild out today, isn't it?

ROSE. *(Pointing at* **FLORA***'s necklace.)* That's a pretty piece. When did you make that?

FLORA. Just the other night. It's a copy of my favorite. The one we sold to…you know.

ROSE. Those are lovely stones.

BLANCHE. They almost look like the real thing. Where did you get them?

FLORA. I can't remember. I just found them.

JACK. *(Penny beginning to drop.)* Where?

FLORA. In the bathroom I think. They were just sitting there. All nineteen of them.

JACK, ROSE, & BLANCHE. Nineteen?

FLORA. I've no idea where they came from.

ROSE. Oh, dear God…

BLANCHE. Do you think…?

JACK. *(Rising.)* Shh. Don't think anything. Don't say anything. Don't even breathe.

> (**JACK** *crosses to* **FLORA***, putting on his glasses.*)

Let me have a look at that.

FLORA. Sure.

> *(Taking off the necklace and handing it to* **JACK***.)*

Here you go. Oh dear, you're not suggesting these are the real diamonds, are you?

JACK. Shh.

> (**JACK** *pulls out his loupe as the others crowd around. He examines the stones. A beat.*)

FLORA. *(Whispering.)* Well?

BLANCHE. Are they real or aren't they?

ROSE. Come on Jack, don't just stand there, say something!

  (The intercom sputters to life.)

VOICE. *(Offstage.)* The shuttle bus to Departure Point has arrived. All those departing for Departure Point, departure is in five minutes.

JACK. *(Looking up at the intercom.)* Oh yeah? Well tell them our departure's been delayed – indefinitely!

FLORA. What?

BLANCHE. *(Overlapping.)* What are you saying, Jack?

ROSE. *(Pointing to* **FLORA***'s necklace.)* You mean – those are the real diamonds?

JACK. They sure are. Every one of them. We're STINKING RICH!

  (They all jump with joy, hooting and hollering and hugging one another.)

Flora, you're a genius! You saved our bacon.

ROSE. *(Overlapping.)* Hooray for Flora!

BLANCHE. *(Overlapping.)* That Effward thought he was so clever – but he was no match for YOU!

JACK. Come here Flora, I've got something for you!

  (He grabs her and plants a big wet kiss on her mouth.)

FLORA. Oh my goodness!

  (Another announcement over the intercom.)

VOICE. *(Offstage.)* Flora Parker, please come to the front desk immediately. Flora Parker to the front desk.

FLORA. Oh. I wonder what that's about.

  (She exits upstage right.)

JACK. I'd love to see the look on Effward's face when he tries to sell that necklace.

BLANCHE. What do you think will happen to them?

ROSE. Well, they won't be completely broke. They do still have that stone stuck inside Nurse Harper.

BLANCHE. Yes, and I hope it ruptures her appendix!

(FLORA re-enters and sits down.)

ROSE. So?

FLORA. So what?

ROSE. What did they want?

FLORA. What did who want?

ROSE. At the desk?

FLORA. Ohh! I forgot.

(She pulls something out of her pocket.)

One of the cleaners found one of my stones.

JACK. Let me take a look at that.

(She gives him the stone. He pulls out his loupe and inspects it.)

FLORA. Nice of them to give it back, eh?

JACK. I'll say – considering it's worth half a million bucks!

FLORA, ROSE, & BLANCHE. What? Ohmigod!

JACK. *(Holding up a diamond.)* It's the twentieth stone. Harper didn't eat it after all.

ROSE. You mean they've been left with nothing?

JACK. That's right!

(Cheers and whoops of joy all around.)

FLORA. What are we going to do with all this money?

BLANCHE. Yes, we've got twice as much as we thought we were going to have.

ROSE. I know! We can set up a website to distribute the extra money to Barney's victims. We can call it Effing Effward dot com.

ALL. Great idea! Perfect! Excellent plan!

(ROSE sits down and starts typing on her iPad.)

JACK. There's something else we've got to do.

BLANCHE. What's that?

JACK. Bring Wilf back home!

FLORA. *(Very enthusiastically.)* Ooh, that's a lovely idea.

(Beat.)

Who's Wilf?

JACK. I'm going to call him right now.

(He starts toward the phone and dials.)

BLANCHE. What are you going to say to him?

JACK. What else?

(Into the phone.)

Hey Wilf – have I got a deal for YOU!

(Everybody cheers and ad-libs joyfully as the curtain falls.)